Six m
Six more indomitable heroines.
One UNIFORMLY HOT! miniseries.

Don't miss a story in Harlequin Blaze's
bestselling miniseries, featuring irresistible soldiers
from all branches of the armed forces.

Don't miss Chance's thrilling story:

COMING UP FOR AIR
by Karen Foley
May 2012

and his twin brother Chase's sexy adventure:

NO GOING BACK
by Karen Foley
July 2012

Uniformly Hot!
The Few. The Proud. The Sexy as Hell.

Blaze™

Dear Reader,

About three years ago, I had the opportunity to sit in the cockpit of a Black Hawk helicopter. With the cyclic stick between my knees and all that powerful technology at my fingertips, I knew I had to create a heroine capable of flying these incredible machines, but also strong enough to hold her own in a male-dominated environment.

Army captain Jenna Larson is a top-notch Black Hawk pilot, but she's sworn never to get romantically involved with another pilot, no matter how sexy he might be. But when she catches sight of Major Chase Rawlins, a hard-bodied special ops commando with a killer smile, she decides he's the one man she wants to see out of uniform and in her bed.

What she doesn't realize is that it's not the professional, no-nonsense Chase that she's been drooling over, but his cocky, devil-may-care twin brother, Chance, an Apache helicopter pilot. Jenna is convinced that she can spend one night with him and then walk away, but their red-hot hookup turns out to be the best sex she's ever had, and she can't stop thinking about him.

Chance Rawlins may just be my favorite hero yet! He has all the qualities that make a military hero irresistible, and I hope you find him hard to forget, too! And if you're wondering about his twin brother…Chase Rawlins will have his own story in July 2012, where he encounters the one woman guaranteed to make him lose control.

Happy reading!

Karen

Karen Foley

COMING UP FOR AIR

TORONTO NEW YORK LONDON
AMSTERDAM PARIS SYDNEY HAMBURG
STOCKHOLM ATHENS TOKYO MILAN MADRID
PRAGUE WARSAW BUDAPEST AUCKLAND

Recycling programs
for this product may
not exist in your area.

ISBN-13: 978-0-373-79686-1

COMING UP FOR AIR

www.Harlequin.com

Printed in U.S.A.

ABOUT THE AUTHOR

Karen Foley is an incurable romantic. When she's not working for the Department of Defense, she's writing sexy romances with strong heroes and happy endings. She lives in Massachusetts with her husband and two daughters, an overgrown puppy and two very spoiled cats. Karen enjoys hearing from her readers. You can find out more about her by visiting www.karenefoley.com.

Books by Karen Foley

HARLEQUIN BLAZE
353—FLYBOY
422—OVERNIGHT SENSATION
451—ABLE-BODIED
504—HOLD ON TO THE NIGHTS
549—BORN ON THE 4TH OF JULY
      "Packing Heat"
563—HOT-BLOODED
596—HEAT OF THE MOMENT
640—DEVIL IN DRESS BLUES

To get the inside scoop on Harlequin Blaze and its talented writers, be sure to check out blazeauthors.com.

All backlist available in ebook. Don't miss any of our special offers. Write to us at the following address for information on our newest releases.

Harlequin Reader Service
U.S.: 3010 Walden Ave., P.O. Box 1325, Buffalo, NY 14269
Canadian: P.O. Box 609, Fort Erie, Ont. L2A 5X3

This book is dedicated to my own personal hero,
John Foley, who didn't have to deploy,
but chose to do so anyway. I'm so proud of you!

_1_

THE WAY TO TELL IF A man was a good lover was to watch
how he danced. Captain Jenna Larson didn't know if
the observation was true, since none of her exes had
enjoyed dancing very much. That should have been her
first clue, since none of them had been exceptional in
bed, either.

A slow country song throbbed through the speakers
at Shooters nightclub, and Jenna could feel the seductive pull of it in her veins. Finishing her beer, she set the
empty bottle down on the bar. She'd told herself a dozen
times since she'd first spotted him that she wasn't going
to look, but her gaze was drawn irresistibly back to the
couple moving slowly across the dance floor. Despite
the crush of people surrounding them, the man guided
his partner effortlessly through the crowd, his hands
holding her with an easy confidence.

He moved with a fluid grace, his body shifting and
sliding in perfect rhythm to the music while accom-
modating his partner's motions. He was lean and fit,
the material of his black shirt stretched taut across the
thrust of his shoulders. His jeans rode low on his hips
and his scuffed cowboy boots lent him extra height.

Watching him dance, Jenna had no doubt that he would be exceptional in bed, completely attuned to his partner's body.

He bent his head to catch something the woman said to him, and then he laughed and drew her closer to the curve of his body, never missing a beat. His teeth were white in his suntanned face and Jenna noted the deep indents in his cheeks when he grinned. As they turned the corner of the dance floor, his gaze slid lazily over the crowd and, for an instant, his eyes met hers and held.

Jenna stared at him over his partner's head, unable to look away. She couldn't recall the last time she'd been so enthralled by a man, military or otherwise. Everything about him commanded her attention, from his built-for-sex body to his lazy, devil-may-care smile. She didn't know the first thing about him, except that he was in the army, assigned to nearby Fort Bragg, just like ninety-five percent of the men in the club that night.

Jenna had caught glimpses of him several times on the army base, and even from a distance he'd captured her attention. Less than two weeks ago, she'd run into him at the local supermarket. Literally, as she'd turned a corner, she'd collided with his shopping cart. He had smiled at her as she'd apologized, and there had been no mistaking the masculine interest in his eyes. In fact, she'd felt him watching her as she'd walked away, and when she'd surreptitiously glanced back at him, he'd grinned shamelessly, making no effort to hide the fact that he was, indeed, ogling her. The knowledge had made her feel shivery and delicious.

Two days later, she'd bumped into him at the post office. Against her better judgment, she'd opened her mouth to introduce herself, but he'd looked right through her, without a hint of recognition or interest. The complete switch had puzzled her, making her wonder if she'd only imagined the heat she'd seen in his eyes just days earlier.

Now, as she watched him, the corners of his lips lifted and he closed one eye in an audacious wink, before smoothly swinging the woman away to the other side of the floor. Jenna realized she had been holding her breath and she let it out in a rush, signaling to the bartender for another beer. The music came to a stop and she peeked back in time to see him give the woman a brief hug before releasing her to rejoin a group of men shooting pool on the far side of the room.

She gave a snort of disdain as she watched the woman pause on the edge of the dance floor and preen for whoever might still be watching her. Wearing too-tight white jeans and a skimpy shirt that exposed her tanned midriff, she was obviously a local. Her long hair was dyed an unnatural shade of red, and she had enough makeup on to qualify as camouflage. But she had a curvy little body, and she smiled at every guy who looked her way, including her dance partner's pool-shooting buddies.

Jenna covertly watched as his friends welcomed his return with nudges and winks. He took it in stride, but while the other guys looked longingly at the redhead's ass when she finally sauntered away, he turned and stared directly at Jenna. She paused, her beer halfway to her lips, and then tipped the bottle toward him in a silent salute before taking a long swallow. He smiled, a slow tilting of his mouth that caused his dimples to emerge, then picked up his cue and turned his attention to the pool table.

"Who're you gawking at?"

Jenna turned to see her copilot and bunk mate, Warrant Officer Laura Costanza, squeeze up to the bar beside her. Together, they had flown three separate training missions during the past twenty-four hours, and had been given the next twenty-four hours off in order to rest and be ready to fly again. Aside from their shared love of flying helicopters, they had little in common, but they'd become close friends in the three years that they'd worked together. Jenna found the other woman's down-to-earth candor both amusing and refreshing. But Jenna also knew that if Laura discovered she'd been lusting after someone, she'd never hear the end of it.

"Nobody," she fibbed. "How was your dance?"

"Had my feet stomped on a couple of times." The younger woman grinned. "No biggie." She shifted her focus to the men shooting pool. "Ah, let me guess. Major Hottie in the black shirt and boots. He *is* drool-worthy."

Jenna shrugged and deliberately turned her back to the dance floor and the pool tables. "He's okay."

Laura laughed. "Yeah, right. Like every female in here doesn't want to jump his bones." She gave a dramatic sigh. "Sadly, he's way above my pay grade. You could always go for it, though. Oh, but I almost forgot—you don't get involved with military guys." She tipped her head as she pretended to consider. "Why is that again?"

Even Laura didn't know the real reason that Jenna avoided men in the military. Her father was a highly decorated Vietnam pilot and had taught Jenna how to fly when she was barely a teenager. But while he might be a legend in the military annals, he'd made her mother's life hell. The same qualities that made him an extraordinary soldier also made him a terrible partner. If she closed her eyes, she could still hear the bitter battles that had waged between him and her mom, mostly over his drinking and his numerous affairs. Jenna's mother would give him an ultimatum, and for a few months he'd actually remain sober. Those were the times that Jenna liked to remember, the long summer days on Cape Cod when she'd help him run his helicopter sightseeing and tour business. She'd logged more flight hours in her teen years than some military pilots did during an entire career. There was no question that her father had been an exceptional flight instructor; he just hadn't been a great husband or father. But he'd been her role model and the center of her young life, and she would have done anything to make him proud. To make him love her. But nothing she did ever seemed good enough. She gave her friend a tolerant look.

"Because I like to keep my private life just that— *private,*" she said. "Getting involved with another soldier is asking for trouble. And how can you tell he's above your pay grade, anyway? Do you know him?"

She and Laura were assigned to a helicopter battalion out of upstate New York, but had been at Fort Bragg, North Carolina, for just over three weeks while they prepared for a six-month deployment to Afghanistan. Their training exercises left little time to socialize or meet other soldiers assigned to the base. The only reason Jenna found herself looking twice at this guy was because she'd been going through a particularly long dry spell. At this point, it didn't take much to fire her engines.

"Well, I don't *know* him," Laura hedged. "I only know his name is Chase Rawlins. He's an army major with Special Ops. His unit deploys in a couple of days. At least, that's what I've heard."

Jenna glanced over her shoulder at the pool table in time to see him smoothly knock a cue ball into a side pocket. Major Hottie, indeed. She'd pegged him for an enlisted guy, which would have made him off-limits, since fraternization between officers and enlisted members was strictly prohibited. But if he was also an officer... Despite her self-denial regarding men in uniform, she couldn't prevent the surge of anticipation she felt at learning he was fair game, should she choose to end her abstinence.

There was just one small problem.

"We leave for Afghanistan in three days," she said glumly. "Even if his unit wasn't deploying, and even if I *was* interested, it's not like I have time to get to know the guy."

Laura raised her eyebrows and took a sip of beer. "Who says you need to get to know him? You're a helicopter pilot. You're genetically predisposed to have meaningless sex."

Jenna laughed, but acknowledged that, for most of the unmarried pilots in her battalion, that was the truth. It was one of the reasons she avoided dating them. One-night stands and short-lived relationships were an accepted way of life for them. Of course, they were also men. Despite the fact she had achieved equality in the cockpit, distinct double standards still existed. If she slept around as much as some of her male counterparts did, she'd find herself the target of some pretty derogatory comments.

Not that Jenna hadn't had her share of hookups. She had. Just not in the past eight months. But she always chose men who had nothing to do with the military;

guys whose worlds were so far removed from her own that there was no chance of them colliding. Guys who couldn't follow her when she returned to base, safe behind the razor-wire fences and security checkpoints.

Of course, that would all change in six months, when both her deployment and her military commitment would end. After a lot of soul-searching, she'd made the decision to get out of the military altogether and return to Cape Cod, where she hoped to help her father run his tour business. He wasn't getting any younger, and she felt a need to spend time with him, to show him that, although she might not be the son he'd always wished for, she'd done okay.

She'd never even considered hooking up with one of her fellow pilots, as gorgeous and funny as some of them were. Most women would kill for the opportunity to peel one of those hotties out of his flight suit, but not Jenna. She'd seen too many relationships crash and burn within the battalion to make that particular mistake. Plus, most of her male colleagues had egos the size of aircraft carriers. From Jenna's perspective, it seemed, no matter how much a female pilot might be liked and respected, ultimately she became the competition. Or the attraction eventually waned, and then the two were stuck working together. She'd seen it happen again and again, and the resulting friction created discomfort for the entire unit.

Thanks, but no thanks.

Despite what Laura had said, Jenna wasn't entirely averse to hooking up with someone in uniform, as long as their respective military careers ensured they wouldn't run into each other during duty hours. The fact that it had been years since she'd been tempted by a fellow soldier didn't mean anything. She just hadn't met anyone who interested her enough to set aside her own number-one rule of engagement.

Until now.

She slid a covert glance at Chase Rawlins as she weighed the risks of getting involved with him, even for one night. At least he wasn't a pilot, and they worked in completely separate units. During the three weeks she'd been at Fort Bragg, she'd never run into him while she'd been working. And in three days, she'd be gone.

"Special Ops, huh?" she asked, tracing a fingertip along the rim of her bottle, considering. If he really was deploying, the likelihood that they would ever see each other again was slim to none. Special Ops commandos kept to themselves and operated under the radar. Their deployments took them to remote locations where few people were aware of their existence. If she decided to get involved with this guy, it would definitely be a hit-and-run maneuver. "So you think I should go for it?"

Laura made a scoffing sound. "Are you *kidding?* The guy is beyond hot. Besides, we're outta here in a couple of days. It's not like you'll ever see him again. And if it makes you feel any better, in six months your commitment to the U.S. Army is over. Once you're back to civilian life, there'll be no chance of running into him again. He's totally checking you out, by the way. No, don't look!"

Jenna groaned. "This is ridiculous. You'd think we were teenagers." After a moment, she slapped both hands decisively on the bar and hopped down from the stool. "I'll take care of this."

"What're you going to do?" Laura asked, her face alight with anticipation.

"Watch and learn, oh young one," Jenna replied, waggling her eyebrows.

"Wait!" Jenna watched as Laura dragged her pocket-book from the back of the bar stool and began rummaging through it. "Here, take this. I always keep extras, just in case." She pushed something into Jenna's hand.

Jenna stared down at the shiny foil packet and gave a huff of astonished laughter. "A *condom?* Seriously, Laura, I don't think—"

"You're right—one's not enough. Take two." She shoved another small packet into Jenna's fingers.

Afraid that someone might see, Jenna stuffed the two condoms into the front pocket of her jeans. "You're unbelievable. This is just a dance."

Laura rolled her eyes. "Yeah, right. And the Beatles were just a band. Now, go!" She made a shooing motion with her hand.

Inside, Jenna's heart was beating fast. She was going to ask him for a dance, and whatever happened after that would be up to him. If they only ended up dancing, it would be no big deal. As she approached the group of men, he straightened and leaned against his cue to watch her, masculine appreciation in his expression. By the time she reached him, the other men had stopped to watch, too.

Jenna halted mere inches from the man, deliberately invading his personal space in what she liked to think of as her first test of compatibility. At five feet, eleven inches tall, she was nearly eye-level with him. She'd learned from experience that some guys found her height a little unsettling, but he seemed unfazed. The warm gleam in his eyes and the hint of a dimple in one cheek made her feel as if her approaching him had been a foregone conclusion, but instead of annoyance, the thought drew a reluctant smile from her.

"Hey," she said in greeting, letting her gaze slide over him.

Up close, the guy was absolutely mouthwatering, from his translucent green eyes, alight with interest, to his square jaw and sensuous smiling mouth. His brown hair was cropped close to his head, but Jenna could see bronze-and-gold glints in the short strands, and guessed he spent a lot of time in the sun, which made sense considering his line of work. He crossed his arms over his chest, and Jenna found herself transfixed by the way the material of his shirt strained over his thick biceps. She swallowed hard and silently acknowledged that she'd be more than a little disappointed if all she got from him was a dance. It seemed every cell in her body suddenly stood at attention, eagerly waiting to obey whatever command he might want to give.

"Hey." He grinned, revealing dimples deep enough to drive a truck into.

Jenna pretended to lean negligently against the pool table, needing something solid to support her as her knees weakened beneath his smile. What had Laura said his first name was? Jenna couldn't think clearly, and hoped her sudden confusion didn't show on her face.

"So, Rawlins," she said, deliberately using just his surname, "You wanna dance?" Her voice sounded both seductive and challenging.

"You bet."

Without taking his eyes from her, he thrust his cue toward the nearest man and caught her hand firmly in his own as he pulled her toward the dance floor. He swung her into his arms, and finally Jenna knew firsthand what it was like to have all that strength and grace surround her. For as long as she could remember, she had struggled to come to terms with her height. Next to other women, she usually felt like a galumphing elephant, but she'd learned a long time ago not to let anyone see her insecurities. Right now, though, despite the fact he was only several inches taller than her, she felt fragile in his arms.

He splayed one hand at the small of her back, while his other held hers captive. There was nothing tentative or polite about the action; it was uncompromisingly confident, bordering on possessive. He maintained just enough space between the framework of their bodies so that they weren't actually touching, but Jenna could feel the heat he generated.

"I haven't seen you in here before." His voice was warm and rich, with a distinctly Texan drawl.

Jenna suppressed a smile, enjoying the easy way he maneuvered her body to match his movements. "That's because I've never been in here before."

He drew back slightly and his eyes narrowed as they traveled leisurely over her features. "Have we met?"

Her breath caught as he suddenly spun her into a neat turn beneath his hand, before bringing her back into his arms. "Oh, wow." She laughed. "Wasn't expecting that." She regained her focus, feeling a little off-balance, steadied only by the warm hand at her back. "Um, no. We haven't actually met, unless you count the time I nearly ran you over in the grocery store last week."

"Ah…" he said meaningfully, as if something had finally clicked. "I knew I'd seen you before." He increased the pressure of his fingers, urging her closer. His warm breath fanned her ear. "So how do you know my name?"

Jenna leaned back enough to stare boldly into his eyes. "I asked."

Their gazes held for a long moment, before his lips curved in a slow smile. He gave a soft laugh of either amusement or admiration and then he eased her body closer, sliding his palm up to rest between her shoulder blades, while he curled his other hand around her fingers and pressed them to his chest. The movement brought her up against his hard contours, and beneath the fingers of her free hand, his shoulder muscles bunched and relaxed.

Jenna's heart beat faster than necessary; too fast for such a slow dance. She was acutely conscious of how well their bodies fit together, their hips perfectly aligned. If she turned her face even fractionally, her lips would brush against the smooth, tanned skin of his neck. She breathed deeply, inhaling a scent that was intensely clean and yet unmistakably masculine. His soap, or a subtle cologne, maybe. Or some crazy, secret pheromone designed purely to arouse the opposite sex. She wanted to rub herself all over him.

"So, do I get to ask your name?" His voice rumbled softly against her ear.

"Hmm." She dragged her mind away from the indecent thoughts swirling through her head to concentrate on his words. "Jenna Larson."

"Are you from around here?"

"No," she replied, thinking of her home on Cape Cod, in Massachusetts. "Just passing through. And you?"

"Originally from Texas, currently assigned to Fort Bragg. But I guess you know that, too, huh?"

Jenna glanced at his face, but his expression gave nothing away. His good looks aside, she liked his easy smile and the warmth that lingered in his eyes when he studied her. "Actually, I didn't know you were from

Texas. But it wasn't difficult to guess you're in the military," she admitted. "Just about every guy in here tonight is. All you have to do is look at the haircuts."

The music came to an end, and Jenna reluctantly allowed Chase to lead her from the dance floor. His gaze flicked to his buddies, still congregated around the pool tables, but he didn't make an immediate move to separate from Jenna.

"Well, thanks for the dance," she said brightly. But when she would have stepped away, he caught her wrist. She turned back, expectant.

"Do you wanna get out of here? Find someplace a little less crowded?" His voice was low…compelling. His eyes searched hers, and Jenna felt her insides churn with anticipation.

"Maybe. What do you have in mind?"

He shrugged and his thumb rubbed the inside of her wrist. "A bottle of wine, an old army blanket and an outstanding view of the jets taking off and landing at Pope Field." His mouth lifted in a lopsided grin. "I happen to know they're doing night maneuvers, and I promise you, it really is spectacular to watch. We don't even need to go on base. There's a field beyond the perimeter that provides a great view."

Jenna considered him closely. Was it possible he didn't realize she was also in the military? Of course, there was no reason why he would; she looked completely ordinary in her jeans and button-down sleeveless top, with her hair loose around her shoulders, and it wasn't as if he could see the dog tags nestled between her breasts. She couldn't blame him for mistaking her for a civilian.

Despite the fact she'd already decided he was fair game, her instincts screamed at her to refuse his offer.

He was too tempting, too confident of his own attraction. She should run as fast as she could in the opposite direction. But the expression in his eyes, combined with the seductive stroke of his finger against her skin, was doing strange things to her common sense. She could no longer remember why she should avoid getting involved with military guys, especially when this one was so damned gorgeous. Not that one night could possibly count as getting involved. After all, she'd be gone in three days. She'd never see him again. She glanced toward the bar, where Laura gave her a thumbs-up.

Chase arched an eyebrow, waiting for her response.

"Well, I do like pinot noir."

2

WITH HER HAND TUCKED firmly into his, Chance Rawlins steered his spoils through the crowded nightclub, intent on getting her outside before she changed her mind. He recalled the incident in the supermarket, when their carts had collided. Normally, he'd have seized the opportunity to chat her up, maybe get a phone number, but she'd turned her cart away so fast he'd wondered if he'd left his fly unzipped.

The last place he'd expected to run into her again was Shooters nightclub, a place normally reserved for junior officers and local gals looking to get some action. Jenna Larson hadn't struck him as falling into the latter category, but he'd been wrong.

Lucky for him.

The only reason he'd been at the club tonight was to give his brother, Chase, a decent send-off. He and his unit of elite special ops commandos were scheduled to deploy to Afghanistan in just two days. Despite the fact that most of his brother's unit had been at the club, ready to raise a beer, Chase hadn't shown up. Probably doing last-minute paperwork, Chance thought. As identical twins, they took their military duties seriously, but that's where any similarity ended. Chase was all business, all the time, whereas Chance had no problem setting his work aside to have a little fun.

He glanced at the woman by his side.

Absolutely no problem whatsoever.

He didn't make a habit of picking women up at clubs, but there was something about this particular woman that made him unable to release her after their dance. She'd aroused an awareness in him, a rush of hot excitement similar to what he felt just before he went out on a dangerous mission. He wasn't about to ignore it.

He held the door open for Jenna, watching as she preceded him down the walkway to the parking lot. The night was warm and clear, with a soft breeze and the sound of night bugs in the surrounding trees. Jenna paused on the pavement, looking around.

"So which car is yours? Wait—don't tell me." She held up a hand to forestall him. "Let me guess."

Chance came to a stop beside her. "You actually think you can guess which car is mine?"

"Sure." She took a step back and pretended to size him up. "If I know your type, it's probably understated and practical, but would need to have a great performance record. Which means it's an expensive model." She searched the lot. "I'm guessing an SUV, maybe a Land Rover or an older Land Cruiser."

Chance gave a soft laugh. She'd just described his brother's vehicle to a T. "Sorry to disappoint you, sweetheart, but you don't know *my type* at all."

She tossed him a determined look. "Just give me a sec, okay?"

Chance spread his arms wide and grinned. "Take as long as you need, darlin'."

He watched as she crossed to the first row of cars

and paused to survey them. While her back was turned, he strolled to where the motorcycles were parked and threw a leg over the leather seat of a low-slung, black Harley. He turned the key, taking a perverse satisfaction in the way she visibly started at the rumble of the deep, throaty engine. Twisting sideways, he withdrew a half helmet from a saddlebag and dangled it on the end of one finger.

"This is yours?" she asked, disbelief written across her face as she walked toward him.

"You still think you know my type?"

To his relief, she merely gave him a tolerant look and accepted the proffered head gear. Chance secured his own helmet, before glancing at Jenna, who stood watching him.

"Climb on," he invited, and rose to a standing position to give her more room. When she'd settled herself behind him, he sat down, acutely aware of her long legs bracketing his hips. "Are you warm enough?" he asked, raising his voice to be heard over the engine. "I have a jacket in the saddlebag. You're welcome to use it."

In answer, she leaned forward and wrapped her arms around his torso. His stomach muscles involuntarily contracted as she splayed her hands over his abdomen, and he could feel the softness of her breasts pressed against his back. Her chin rested on his shoulder as she spoke directly into his ear, her warm breath fanning his cheek.

"I'm sure I'll be warm enough."

Chance nearly groaned, his body registering the heat of her palms and the pressure of her thighs, aware of every breath she drew. He eased the bike backward out of the parking spot and then accelerated toward the open road, gratified when she clutched at him and hung on even tighter. From the moment he'd spotted her sitting at the bar, she'd intrigued him. She stood out from the other women in the club, and not just because of her height.

He liked her long, slim body and the way she seemed completely comfortable in her own skin. She didn't slouch or try to disguise the fact that she stood a head taller than most other women. She walked with the loose-limbed gait of an athlete, but Chance could easily envision her wearing an elegant evening gown... or better yet, some sexy number involving a thong and thigh-high, sheer stockings that emphasized the length of her legs. She wore a minimal amount of makeup, and her hair hung in sleek waves around her face, the lights of the club picking out the red highlights in the thick, brown tresses. She looked reserved and unapproachable, almost haughty.

Until she looked at him.

Then her expression turned hungry. Like she knew what she wanted and to hell with anyone who stood in her way.

Good thing she was just passing through. Her eyes, cool and carnal, made him want to do decadent things with her. He itched to bury his hands in her hair and muss the sleek waves. He wanted to wipe the sheen of gloss from her lips with his mouth. He wanted those mile-long legs wrapped around his waist.

He couldn't recall the last time he'd had such a visceral response to a woman. He couldn't even blame it on alcohol, since he'd had only one beer. But he'd seen the way the other guys eyeballed her, and he'd been gripped with an overwhelming need to keep her to himself, away from the loud music and artificial atmosphere of the club. He didn't need to get any crazy ideas about seeing her again after tonight, which should have made him feel relieved. But the thought of *not* seeing her again roused an uncomfortable, unfamiliar emotion that felt suspiciously like regret. And that alone was enough to convince him that he shouldn't see her again.

They roared along the familiar streets with her hugging his back until they came to a convenience store. Pulling the Harley up to the curb, he turned off the engine and removed his helmet.

"I'll be right back," he promised, easing himself from the bike. Without her warmth surrounding him, he felt chilled.

Inside the shop, he selected a bottle of wine from the cooler and helped himself to a couple of paper cups from the coffee bar. When he came back out, Jenna had scooted forward on the seat and had her hands firmly on the handle-grips. Her long legs easily reached the ground and she looked as if she belonged there. His rampant imagination conjured up images of her lounging back on the Harley wearing nothing but a smile and a pair of four-inch stilettos.

"Mind if I drive?" she asked, a challenging glint in her eyes.

Chance stopped in his tracks. "Do you know how?"

She shrugged. "How hard can it be?"

He laughed as he came forward and stashed the bottle and cups inside one of the saddlebags. "Maybe another time."

"What? Do you have a problem riding behind a woman?" she asked. Her tone was light, but Chance paused, sensing something more in her words.

He straightened and gave her a slow grin. "Actually, no, I don't. In fact, it's one of my favorite positions."

Even in the darkness, Chance didn't miss how her eyes assessed him. After a moment, she slid back, relinquishing the driver's position. Leaning forward, he braced one hand on the seat by her hip and the other on the handlebar. "Listen, if you had a motorcycle endorsement on your license, and if I knew for a fact you were completely sober and if I thought you could actually handle the weight of the bike *and* a passenger, I'd have no problem letting you drive, okay?"

Her fingers paused on the fastening of her helmet and her eyes narrowed as she looked at him. "Really?"

"Really. But for now, let me take care of it." He traced a thumb along the soft curve of her jaw. "Besides, you feel good behind me."

Without waiting for a response, he eased himself onto the bike, smiling as her arms came back around him. Within minutes, they reached a narrow road that meandered through the dark trees and finally emerged into a wide field. Directly in front of them lay the lights of Pope airfield, so close that Chance could see the shadowy figures of the controllers in the tower.

He drew the bike to a stop in the tall grass and waited for Jenna to dismount. Fireflies flickered in the darkness, and the sound of crickets filled the air.

"Wow," she said, pulling her helmet off and staring at the airstrip. "This is amazing. We're like fifty feet from the end of the runway."

They were actually more than five hundred feet from the runway, but Chance didn't disagree with her. Once the planes started to come in, the distance wouldn't matter. Hanging their helmets from the handlebars, he dug through the saddlebags and withdrew a wool army blanket and the bottle of wine.

"C'mon, I'll spread the blanket over here," he said,

tromping on the tall grass to flatten it. He opened the blanket and flapped it onto the ground, before sitting down. Jenna stood near the motorcycle, watching him. He patted the blanket invitingly. "C'mon. I promise not to bite."

"Does anyone ever come out here?"

He shrugged. "Not that I know of. At least, I've never seen anyone else out here." He indicated the woods behind them. "The road dead ends at an electrical service station about a quarter mile that way, so there's no reason for anyone to come out here." He smiled at her through the darkness. "But if there was, you're safe with me."

As she crossed to where he sat, Chance opened the wine and poured some into the paper cups, handing one to her as she lowered herself on the blanket beside him. Sitting cross-legged, she stared up at the sky. A brilliant light hung suspended in the distance, like an overly bright star signaling an incoming aircraft.

"Here comes one now," she said, and took a sip of her wine before leaning over to look more closely at the bottle. "Mmm. Is this a pinot noir? You were actually listening to me."

Chance nodded and took an appreciative sip. "Did I do good?"

She slanted an amused glance in his direction. "You've done okay. So far."

"Then I'll have to try harder," he replied with a soft laugh. "Look, here she comes."

Jenna turned her attention toward the incoming aircraft. Chance could hear the engines rev as the pilot throttled back.

"Looks like a cargo plane," Jenna mused as it began its final descent.

"Yep. A C-130 Hercules. The 4th Brigade is doing a night jump, so this baby just dropped them off."

As the plane drew closer, it appeared that it would fly directly over the spot where they sat. The aircraft came in low, its jets deafening on the night air. The vibration was enough that Chance felt it in his chest, and he looked at Jenna in time to see her mouth form a soundless "oh" of amazement as the big bird screamed over their heads. Even in the indistinct light, he could see the enjoyment on her face and felt a ridiculous sense of pleasure that he'd been responsible for putting it there.

"Wow," she exclaimed, after the C-130 touched down. "That was freaking amazing! I don't think I've ever watched a landing from quite this perspective."

"The show's not over yet. Look." Chance directed her attention to a helipad on the far side of the runway. "They'll send a brigade of Black Hawks out to extract the paratroopers from the jump site."

As the roar of the C-130 engines faded, Chance could hear the *thwap-thwap* of the helicopter rotors churning to life. The first bird lifted slowly into the air and hovered for a brief moment, silhouetted against the night sky before accelerating forward, directly above the spot where they sat.

Chance lay flat on his back and drew Jenna down beside him, turning his head to watch her as five Black Hawks thundered above them, the downward wash from their rotors stirring the grass and blowing Jenna's hair around her face.

"Oh, man, I love that sound!" She shifted on the blanket to look at him, laughing, and Chance felt his breath catch.

Setting his cup of wine aside, he rose up on one

elbow and used his free hand to tug a strand of hair loose from the corner of her mouth, where it had caught.

"Did you enjoy that?" he asked, when the racket of the helicopters had faded.

She gazed up at him, still smiling. "Oh, yeah."

Her eyes were mysterious in the dim light, her mouth soft and lush. Her dark hair fanned out on the blanket beneath her head and Chance twined a silky lock of it around his finger. Beneath her blouse, her breasts rose and fell in an agitated way, betraying the fact that she wasn't nearly as relaxed as she pretended to be.

"So what made you go to Shooters tonight?" he asked, idly rubbing the strand of hair between his fingers.

She made a small, shrugging motion. "I went with a friend, more out of boredom than anything else."

He fastened his gaze on her mouth. "And are you bored now?"

"Getting there," she said huskily, and moistened her lips. "You might have to do something about that. Any ideas?"

"Well, for starters, I really want to kiss you," he confessed in a husky voice, studying her face.

"Thank God," she breathed. Reaching up, she slid a hand to the back of his head and drew him down to her.

CHASE RAWLINS CLEARLY knew how to kiss, and enjoyed doing it. He leaned over her, cupping her face in his palm as his mouth leisurely explored hers. His lips were warm and firm and he tormented her with soft, lingering kisses as his thumb caressed her cheek.

Jenna really had gone too long without sex. What

other reason could there be for the way her blood hummed through her veins, or the way his touch did crazy things to her already heightened senses? She was acutely conscious of how warm and solid he felt against her body. He tasted faintly of wine, and she breathed in the intoxicating blend of his aftershave, the warm, fusty odor of the woolen blanket and the crisp scent of the crushed grass beneath them. She wanted to devour him, but he kept his kisses frustratingly sweet, teasing her, but not giving her what she craved.

"Open your mouth," she breathed against his lips, desperate to taste him.

He made a noise, something between a groan and sigh, and then his tongue was in her mouth, sliding against hers and ratcheting up her need. The hot, moist kiss triggered an answering rush of dampness between her thighs. She wanted to throw a leg across his hips and press herself against him. Instead, she squeezed her knees together and told herself to slow down. But when he deepened the kiss, Jenna couldn't prevent sliding her arms around his broad shoulders and arching against him, telling him without words that she wanted more.

He grunted softly in approval, and before she knew what he intended, he rolled onto his back, pulling her with him until she lay sprawled across his chest, her legs tangled with his. Gasping, she eased away enough to look down into his face. In the indistinct light, his eyes seemed to glow in his tanned face, and his breathing came in hard pants.

"I'm too heavy for you," Jenna protested. But when she would have pushed away, he restrained her.

"Are you kidding?" He sounded astonished. "You feel great."

As if to emphasize his words, he thrust his fingers

into her hair where it hung loose around her face and drew her back down, covering her mouth with his own. Jenna resisted for about a fraction of a second before the heat of his kiss caused her to melt against him. When he wedged a hard thigh between her legs, she instinctively rode it, savoring the friction against her center, where she pulsed hotly. He speared her tongue with his, in concert with the rocking of her hips against his leg. The sensation was amazing, but she wanted more.

Pulling back, Jenna straddled him. He shifted beneath her, until she was pressed fully against the hard ridge of his arousal.

"Oh, man, you feel good," she said, bracing her hands on his chest and moving reflexively back and forth. The intimate contact created a fresh flood of moisture to saturate her panties, and her nipples felt tight and achy.

As if he knew what she needed, he reached up and covered her breasts with his hands. All the air escaped from her lungs in a soft rush of pleasure. Her back arched as his thumbs stroked across the distended nipples.

She was glad now that while he'd been in the store buying the wine, she'd slipped her dog tags off and pushed them into the pocket of her jeans. There was no doubt in her mind that this was going to get very intimate, very quickly. She could almost guess how he might respond if he saw the telltale evidence of her military service, and she didn't need to have him ruin the moment by asking questions. She'd learned from experience that most men found her job as threatening as her height, so she avoided talking about it whenever possible.

Only her father seemed less than impressed with her chosen career. Part of the reason she'd opted to become an army helicopter pilot was to make him proud, although she'd never admit to him how much his opinion mattered, or how everything she did and even how she felt about other pilots could be traced right back to him. She could barely admit it to herself. She was a more than competent pilot, she knew that, yet she couldn't seem to shake the sense that, no matter how good she was, she'd never be quite good enough. She'd worked twice as hard as any of the guys in her unit, and had achieved just as much, so why did she feel as if she was a disappointment to her father? And why did it matter so much? Aside from teaching her how to fly helicopters, he'd hardly taken any notice of her. She didn't owe him anything.

"Tell me what you want," he rasped. His face was taut as he watched her. "What you like."

The small part of Jenna's brain that still functioned knew she should stop, but the sensations coursing through her body were too intense. She needed more of the delicious contact. Covering his hands with her own, she encouraged his caresses even as she angled her hips for optimum friction.

"I like this," she assured him. Her voice sounded husky and unfamiliar, even to herself. "But I want more."

When her hands moved to the buckle of his belt, he made a sound like a helpless groan and caught her wrists.

"Wait."

Jenna's hands stilled. His features were all hard angles in the dim light and she silently berated herself for having moved too fast. When would she learn that not all men appreciated women who took the initiative? "What is it?"

"I want you to know that I didn't bring you out here for this. I mean, I'd hoped, of course—" He gave her a lopsided grin. "But it wasn't something I'd planned on. I just wanted you to know."

Jenna felt a smile tug at her mouth. She hadn't expected him to be so considerate, although she should have guessed. After all, she'd seen him dance. "Okay... so does this mean you want me to stop?"

"Hell, no!" He released her wrists. "But it's only fair I tell you that we might not see each other again after tonight. So if that bothers you..."

"It doesn't," she assured him. "Like I said before, I'm only here for a few days, and then I'll be gone." She paused meaningfully. "So, unless you're married or something..."

He laughed softly and raised his ringless hands for her inspection. "No wife. No fiancée. No girlfriend."

"Then no worries, because I'm not looking for any promises. Your job is dangerous, and you can never be sure where you're going to be from one day to the next. Trust me, I get it. Not exactly conducive to a relationship, right?"

"Right..."

She heard the cautious agreement in his voice, and wondered if she'd made another faux pas. Maybe he didn't want her to know that he was with special ops. Some of those guys were funny about revealing their connection to the black world of covert operations. But she really did get it, because her own career made it difficult for her to establish any romantic ties.

"All I'm trying to say is that I'm okay with keeping this casual," she clarified. "No strings. No commitments." Leaning down, she put her mouth next to his ear and lowered her voice to a sultry whisper. "No problem."

3

CHANCE COULDN'T THINK of one damn reason to argue with her, not when her heat scorched him through his jeans and her hands were at his belt, finishing the task he'd interrupted just moments earlier. He'd been honest with her. He'd told her that whatever they shared wouldn't extend beyond tonight, and she'd been okay with it. More than okay, really. He should feel a little insulted that she was so okay with not seeing him again, but suddenly he couldn't think about much beyond the feel of her fingers unzipping his jeans and tentatively stroking him beneath the fabric of his boxers.

"You're so hard," she breathed.

Oh, yeah.

"You're sure—"

"Shh." She lay her fingers over his mouth. "You talk too much."

As if to emphasize her point, she leaned down and covered his lips with her own, sliding her tongue against his. Chance wanted to groan with pleasure. He buried his fingers in her hair and angled her face for better access, luxuriating in the damp silk of her mouth. She made a small noise in her throat and shifted so that she could reach between their bodies and cover his straining erection with her hand. The heat of her palm through the thin cotton had him pushing upward, instinctively seeking more of the erotic contact.

"Mmm," she murmured approvingly. "You like that?"

Chance managed to grunt a reply, and then ceased to think altogether when she slipped a hand inside the waistband of his boxers and curled her fingers around him. He couldn't recall the last time he'd been so aroused so quickly. Of course, he hadn't been with anyone in more than six months, and that kind of deprivation had a way of ratcheting up your libido. But Chance suspected that even if he hadn't gone through a recent dry spell, he'd have a tough time resisting Jenna Larson. Everything about her turned him on. When she began to rhythmically slide her hand along his length, he groaned loudly and reached down to wrap a restraining hand around her wrist.

"Darlin'," he panted, "you need to slow down, or this is going to be over a whole lot quicker than either of us wants."

To both his regret and relief, Jenna released him.

"Sorry," she whispered against his lips, "but I really want to touch you."

She raised herself to a sitting position and ran her palms over the planes of his chest, her expression so sexy that Chance knew if she touched him again the way she just had, he'd be a goner. He didn't protest when she began unfastening the buttons on his shirt and then tugged the fabric free from his waistband until he was exposed to her greedy gaze.

"Holy shit," she muttered, and stroked a fingertip down the shallow groove that bisected his torso until she encountered the tip of his erection where it protruded above the waistband of his boxers. "It's like you've been…airbrushed. Only, better."

Chance gave a huff of laughter, grateful for the long hours he'd spent in physical training. He kept his body in prime condition, not just because the army required it, but because he and his brother had an ongoing rivalry over which of them was in better shape. With his rigorous special ops training, Chase usually kicked his ass in that department, but Chance suddenly didn't care. If Jenna Larson liked what she saw, that was more than good enough for him.

She still straddled his hips, and when she swirled the tip of her finger over the head of his penis, Chance groaned and strained upward.

"Okay, that's enough," he growled softly. "My turn."

Without giving her time to protest, he slid her to one side of the blanket and sat up, bending forward to yank his boots off and toss them aside. Her eyes never left him as he peeled his shirt away and spread it out on the blanket behind him, before he stood and swiftly shed his jeans. Finally, when all he wore were his boxers, he dropped back onto the blanket and turned to Jenna.

"That's better," he murmured, and scooted closer until mere inches separated them. Bracing himself on his forearm, he undid the first button of her blouse, and then the second. In the dim light, he could just make out the lacy edge of her bra. His fingers paused over the third button, and he slanted her a questioning look.

"Don't stop now," she murmured, and a hint of a smile curved her lips. Beneath his hand, Chance could feel the frantic, unsteady beat of her heart.

He slid a hand beneath the fall of her hair and dipped his head to cover her lips once more. She sighed into his mouth and her hand forged a molten trail along his rib cage and over his hip to boldly cup his butt and urge him closer.

Chance resisted the urge to grind against her, and instead focused on slowly unbuttoning her blouse as he explored her mouth with his tongue. When the fabric fell open beneath his fingers, he raised his head to admire the exposed swell of soft flesh beneath the lacy bra and the long, slender length of her waist.

"Gorgeous," he muttered, and stroked the back of his fingers across the satiny skin, watching in fascination as her stomach muscles contracted beneath his touch. When he reached the waistband of her jeans, he didn't wait for her permission, but flicked the button open and drew the zipper down in one easy movement. In the splayed vee of denim, he could just make out the top edge of her panties, and was helpless to prevent himself from laying his palm against her smooth abdomen. He wanted to plant his mouth there. Christ, he wanted to kiss her everywhere. He wanted to lick her skin, breathe in her scent and feel her softness against his palms. He dragged in a deep breath and forced himself to slow down.

Jenna made a small sound of frustration, and then her hands were there, pushing her jeans over her hips, even as she kicked her sandals free from her feet. Chance watched, mesmerized, as her long legs were exposed, and then she was gloriously bare except for the scrap of lace at her crotch, gleaming white in the darkness.

She rolled toward him, hitching one slim thigh over his leg, and running her hand along his bare skin. With a muffled groan, he gathered her fully against him, his hands smoothing over her back to survey the dips and curves of her shoulder blades and spine. He buried his face in her neck and inhaled her fragrance. She was slim and supple, and when he drew a hand along the back of her thigh and angled her leg higher over his hip, she made an inarticulate sound of pleasure in her throat and pressed her center against his aching cock. She planted hot, moist kisses against his neck and jaw, and her hands were everywhere, exploring his body with an urgency that told him just how aroused she was. Sliding a hand between their bodies, he cupped her through the scrap of silk.

Heat. Moisture. Incredible softness.

Easing the fabric to one side, he stroked a finger along her slick cleft. She gave a strangled cry of pleasure and her hips bucked sharply.

Lust slammed into him with the force of a freight train.

Jenna moaned softly and pushed herself against his fingers, drenching them with the evidence of her arousal. Chance's cock grew even stiffer, and with a rough sound of need, he rolled her onto her back and settled himself between her splayed thighs, rocking hard against her core. Jenna groaned loudly and grabbed the back of his head, slanting her mouth over his in a deep, openmouthed kiss that sent bolts of white-hot flame straight to his balls. He had a hard time focusing on anything except how bad he wanted to be inside her. He needed to slow down.

Breaking the kiss, he pushed her bra down beneath her breasts, and then covered one plump mound with his hand and rubbed his thumb across the distended tip.

"Oh, God. That feels so good," she gasped, and arched upward, rubbing herself along the length of his erection. "Help me take these off."

Chance turned his face to watch as she pushed her panties down and used her feet to kick them free. In the dim light, he could just make out the dark triangle of curls at the apex of her thighs, and then she was pulling him back on top of her, settling him into the cradle of her hips so that his heavy erection rested against her mons.

"Where were we?" she asked in a sultry whisper.

"Right here," he muttered.

Dipping his head, Chance wrapped his lips around one nipple, drawing it into his mouth as he suckled it. Jenna speared her fingers through his hair and held his head to her breast, her breathing coming in uneven pants. He laved her breast with his tongue while he continued to cup and stroke her other breast with his free hand. He was acutely conscious of her nudity as she squirmed desperately beneath him, bracing one heel on the back of his thigh and rubbing herself against his rigid arousal. But when she reached between their bodies and gripped him in her hand, he nearly came apart.

"Jesus!" He dragged his mouth from her breast and looked down to see her stroking the smooth head of his penis against her slippery clitoris. He was breathing hard, just barely keeping himself in check, but when he looked back at Jenna's face, he saw she'd already lost it. Her eyes were half-closed, her expression one of pleasure-pain as she rotated her hips against his swollen flesh. As Chance watched, enthralled, she shuddered lightly and cried out, bucking against him as her orgasm washed over her. But when she would have pushed him inside herself, a small vestige of sanity made him grasp her wrist, and he drew marginally away from her.

Her eyes opened and she looked up at him, dazed. "What's wrong?" Her words were thick. "Don't you want to?"

Her fingers were still wrapped around his shaft, squeezing him at the base, and it took all his restraint not to spill himself in her hand. She looked like every erotic fantasy he'd ever had, sprawled beneath him with her breasts pushed up, her expression one of pure sexual desire as she held his throbbing dick in her hand.

"I'm not wearing a condom," he said through gritted teeth.

"Oh, shit." She abruptly released him.

Chance sucked in a lungful of air as he struggled for control, using the opportunity to shuck his boxers completely. Propping herself on one elbow, Jenna grabbed her discarded jeans and began fishing through the pockets until, with a frustrated growl, she gave the pants a vigorous shake. Chance heard the tinkle of something metallic hit the blanket, and then two small foil squares plopped onto her stomach.

He looked at her in disbelief. "You carry condoms in your pocket?"

Even in the darkness, he saw the color that washed into her face. "Not me—my friend," she explained. "She gave them to me earlier."

"Give her a kiss for me when you see her," he said, and tore one of the wrappers open with his teeth.

When he would have rolled the sheath over himself, Jenna's hands were there to do it for him. Then he was easing himself into her, inch by exquisite inch, while she made small, feminine sounds of pleasure and rocked her hips to meet him. When he was fully seated in her tightness, he paused and struggled for control. She was hot and wet and unbelievably snug, and he could feel the walls of her inner muscles clenching him. The condom had thankfully dulled his sensitized nerve endings, but only enough that he was able to push inside her without coming. He was completely jacked for her. Slowly, he withdrew and then sank back into her, feeling her muscles squeezing him. He groaned as pressure gathered at the base of his spine.

"Christ, you feel good," he muttered, and thrust again. "I want you to come again, this time with me in you."

"Oh, God," she panted as he increased his pace, pulling out until he was almost free from her body, and then plunging back in. "Oh, yeah…"

Reaching down, he caught her leg behind the knee and pushed it back, bracing himself on one hand so that he could watch the spot where they were joined. The sight of his cock disappearing into her body was incredibly arousing, and he knew he wasn't far from his own orgasm.

"Come for me," he demanded softly, and releasing her leg, he reached between their bodies to stroke her with his thumb, sliding his finger over the small, slick nub of flesh. She gave a sharp cry of pleasure and lifted her head to watch. Her entire body trembled. Chance quickened his thrusts as he stroked her, feeling his balls tighten painfully with the need for release.

He was only vaguely aware of the distant *thwap-thwap* of helicopter rotors approaching, signaling the return of the Black Hawks from their night mission. At that moment, an entire squadron of attack choppers could have landed beside them and he would have been helpless to react. Nothing existed but the woman beneath him and the sharp, hot arousal that spiraled through him.

Jenna's expression was taut, her eyes hazy and un-focused as she raised her gaze to his, and he knew the precise instant when she teetered on the brink of climax and then plummeted over the edge. At the same time, the roar of helicopter engines became deafening as the battalion of Black Hawks flew directly overhead, churning up wind and grass, and causing Chance's entire body to thrum with vibration. He heard himself give a hoarse shout as he came in a blinding, white-hot rush of pleasure that caused his spine to bow and his molars to ache. Several long moments later, when all he could hear were the surrounding crickets and his own harsh breathing, he became aware of Jenna's fingers tracing lazy patterns across his lower back, and he raised his head to peer at her.

"You okay?" His voice sounded raspy.

She turned her face and planted a damp kiss against his mouth. Her breath was warm and came in soft pants against his skin. "Better than okay." She gave a soft laugh. "That was freaking amazing. In fact, I think that may have qualified as the best sex of my life. *Two orgasms...* Who would have thought?"

Chance smiled against her neck, absurdly pleased by her words and knowing that sex with Jenna Larson had definitely been the best he'd ever had. The only problem was he wanted more.

"Do you think they saw us?"

"Who?" He was having trouble getting his head together, and it took a minute for her words to register. The sound of rotors had dimmed to a distant whir, and then they stopped altogether. "You mean, the helos? No way. They didn't have their spotlights on, and their attention would have been focused on the landing pad, and not on the field. Besides, it's too dark."

"What if the pilots were wearing night-vision goggles?"

Withdrawing from the warmth of her body, Chance neatly disposed of the condom before reclining back on the blanket and pulling Jenna snugly against his side. "*If* the pilots were wearing night-vision goggles, and *if* they spotted us, then all they saw was my backside." He pressed a kiss against her temple. "Don't worry."

Jenna made an incoherent sound that told him she wasn't completely reassured, but before Chance could soothe her further, something hard and sharp dug into his hip. Reaching beneath him, he retrieved the offending object. He held it up, staring at it in bemusement. A set of military dog tags dangled from the end of his fingers, and since his own tags were fastened securely around his neck, he knew they didn't belong to him. He turned to Jenna in disbelief.

"Are these yours?"

"What if they are?" Her voice sounded defensive.

"Jesus. Why didn't you tell me you were active duty?"

"Does it matter?" Pulling her bra into place, she snatched the necklace from his hand and dropped the chain over her head so that the tags nestled between her breasts. Pulling away from Chance, she sat up and fished around on the blanket until she found her panties.

"Goddamn right, it matters," Chance retorted, watching as she stood up to pull them on. Even as his thoughts raced through the various—and unpleasant—implications of what this could mean, he couldn't help but admire her lithe form as she quickly got dressed. Unless she was a commissioned officer, he could get into serious trouble for fraternization, since contact with enlisted members was strictly prohibited. "Please tell me you're not enlisted."

She paused long enough to give him a tolerant look, and then balled up his discarded boxers and threw them at his chest. "Don't worry. I may be a sucker for a handsome face, but I'm not completely brainless. I'm an army captain."

Chance refrained from making the obvious rejoinder, too floored by her admission to crack any kind of joke. He could only stare stupidly at her. He definitely hadn't seen this one coming. "So what is it that you do?" he finally managed. "What unit are you assigned to?"

She paused in buttoning her blouse and looked across the meadow and razor-wire fences to the runway and helicopter landing area. "See those Black Hawks? That's my unit. I'm with the 10th Combat Aviation Brigade out of Fort Drum. If I hadn't already exceeded my flying hours for the day, I would have been piloting one of those birds to the extraction site."

For a moment, Chance was too stunned to speak. When he finally found his voice, it sounded strained. "You're a Black Hawk *pilot?*"

Jenna thrust her long legs into her jeans and pulled them up, watching him warily. "Do you have a problem with that?"

"Hell, no," Chance assured her as he stood up and began to gather his own clothing. "I think it's great! I mean that sincerely. Really." He paused and scrubbed a hand hard over his face and laughed softly. *A freaking pilot.* Who would have thought? "You just surprised me, that's all. As a matter of fact, I'm—"

"I know what they say about pilots," she interrupted, "and most of the time, I'm in total agreement."

Chance looked at her, puzzled. "What do they say about pilots?"

She shrugged and sat down on the blanket. Reaching for the bottle of wine, she poured them both a little more. "How do you know if you're halfway through a date with a pilot?" She gave him an overly bright smile. "Because he—or in my case, *she*—says *'That's enough about flying. Let's talk about me!'*"

Chance laughed and lowered himself down beside her. "You haven't talked about flying once tonight, but if you'd like, we can talk about you. In fact, *you* are quickly becoming my new favorite subject."

He watched her closely in the indistinct light, wishing he could read the expression in her eyes. He knew he was staring, but he couldn't help it. Who would have guessed that she was a freaking helicopter pilot? It shouldn't have mattered, but for him it made all the difference.

She took a sip of wine, smiling at him from over the rim of the cup. "How do you know when there's a pilot at your party?"

Chance had heard the joke countless times, but he shrugged. "I don't know. How?"

"He'll tell you. How many pilots does it take to change a lightbulb?" She waited, but when Chance didn't respond, she continued. "Just one. He holds the lightbulb, while the world revolves around him."

"Wow." Chance gave a small huff of laughter. "Sounds like you don't think very highly of your fellow pilots."

"Oh, no. That's where you're wrong. I have a huge amount of respect for what they do when they're in the cockpit. They're some of the bravest, most talented guys I know." She grimaced. "It's what they do the rest of the time that bugs me."

"Clarify, please."

Jenna shrugged. "They're incapable of handling a committed relationship. If they have to consider anyone other than themselves, they fail. Basically, they're shallow, narcissistic, egotistical, arrogant—" She broke off abruptly. "Well, you get the picture."

Chance blew out a hard breath. Her words both disturbed and disappointed him. "So...you dated a pilot and he turned out to be a self-centered jackass, is that it?"

To his surprise, Jenna shook her head. "No way. My opinions are based strictly on a lifetime of observation. I've never actually dated another pilot. In fact, I make it a point to steer clear of them—at least, romantically."

Chance felt something fist low in his gut. "Oh, yeah? I'd think you'd be happy to have someone who understands what it is you do. Someone who really gets it."

"Ha! The only thing they want to *get* is laid."

"So I guess you're performing true to form, then, huh?" Chance couldn't keep the bitterness out of his voice.

"What do you mean?"

"I mean, look at you...you're a pilot. What makes you so different from the guys? You clearly wanted to get laid, and you succeeded." He gave her a terse smile. "Glad to have been of service, ma'am."

He began buttoning his shirt, refusing to look at her, because if he did, she might see something in his eyes that he was trying really hard to hide.

Regret. Disappointment.

He shouldn't care what her motives were for being with him. It wasn't as if he was planning on seeing her again. They'd agreed that this wasn't going to be anything more than a onetime hookup. No strings. No commitments. So why did he feel so miserable?

Jenna sighed. Reaching out, she lay a hand on his arm. "Look, it wasn't like that, okay?" She gave a rueful laugh. "To your credit, I broke my own rules when I agreed to come out here with you. My number-one rule is to never sleep with a pilot, so at least I didn't break that rule, thank God. But I generally try not to get involved with anyone in the military, period. I don't like to mix business with pleasure."

The woman didn't have the first clue what he did for a living. Chance's first instinct was to tell her, just so he could see her response. Instead, he gave a snort and finished fastening his shirt. He didn't trust himself to look at her. "I'm flattered. Really."

She made a sound of frustration. "I'm not trying to *flatter* you—"

"Do the guys in your battalion have any clue how you feel about them?" he asked, cutting her off. He knew he sounded bitter, but he couldn't stop himself. "Do they realize what a low opinion you have of them?"

Even in the darkness, he could see how taken aback she was. "Just because I prefer not to sleep with them doesn't mean I have a low opinion of them. And why are you getting upset about this? Trust me, they have such high opinions of themselves that what I think doesn't even register on their ego-meters."

"Right." Chance pushed himself to his feet and began scooping up their things, forcing her to scoot off the blanket so that he could roll it into an untidy ball and stuff it into his saddlebag. "It's getting late. I'll take you back to the club or drive you home. Whichever you prefer."

He didn't look at Jenna, but concentrated on packing up instead. He felt like he'd just made a crash landing after an exceptionally spectacular flight, and now his only hope was that he could walk away from the wreckage unscathed. He wasn't going to argue with her and ruin what had, up until a few moments ago, been the best night he'd spent in a very long time. She was entitled to her opinions and it wasn't like they were ever going to see each other again. Even if he *had* wanted to ask her out, once she discovered what he did for a living, she'd be gone from his life faster than a Hellfire missile.

Better to let her believe that her record was untarnished. Because after hearing her opinions about pilots, there was no way in hell he was going to tell her that she'd broken her own number-one rule. She'd just had the best sex of her life with an Apache helicopter pilot. Boo-rah.

4

Two months later—Nuristan Province, Afghanistan

JENNA BROUGHT THE BLACK Hawk in low and fast, her eyes sweeping the narrow mountain pass for any signs of insurgency. Behind her, in the open door of the cabin, Specialist Leeann Baker squeezed off several magazines as a warning to deter any possible ambush. Once through the pass, Jenna would have a visual on Forward Operating Base Kalagush, where her current passengers would disembark and she would collect another group bound for Kabul Air Base.

The stark valley, surrounded on all sides by the naked, forbidding peaks of the Hindu Kush mountains, always gave Jenna the shivers. No matter how many times she flew this particular route, she couldn't shake the sense that she'd stumbled into an episode of *The Land That Time Forgot*. If a prehistoric pterodactyl suddenly took wing from the nearby crags, she wouldn't have been at all surprised.

Fortunately, the only predatory birds in the nearby airspace were the second Black Hawk that flew hard on her right flank and the fully manned Apache attack helicopter that provided cover from above. Even with the armed escorts, she wouldn't breathe easy until they were on the ground at Kalagush. They'd stay just long enough to refuel and reload passengers, before they made the return trip to Kabul Air Base, arriving before darkness fell.

In the seat beside her, so close that their elbows nearly touched, Warrant Officer Laura Costanza radioed their position to the control tower at the remote base. Jenna listened carefully to the instructions provided by the tower and checked the coordinates on the multifunctional display. She'd been flying for nearly five hours, and now she feathered the cyclic stick between her knees while simultaneously working the collective to control her angle of descent.

The mountain pass opened up, and spread out on the desolate wasteland beneath her was the sprawling complex of Forward Operating Base Kalagush, a small patch of Western civilization smack in the middle of the unforgiving terrain of northern Afghanistan. Several minutes later, Jenna brought the helicopter to a smooth landing on the helipad and shut the rotors down.

"Welcome to Kalagush," she shouted to the soldiers as they gathered their gear together in the cabin. "Enjoy your stay and thank you for flying with the U.S. Army. We know you have no other options, but we still appreciate your business."

As always, her comments drew laughs and ribald comments from the men as they jumped down from the helicopter and made their way across the tarmac to their new duty station.

"And they say women can't park!" one of the soldiers said, grinning at her as he climbed out. "Nice flying, ma'am!"

"How long do we have?" she asked Laura, as she shut everything down and completed her flight paperwork.

Laura flipped open a flight book and consulted her watch. "Twenty minutes to unload, refuel, reload and lift off."

Switching off her headset, Jenna removed her helmet and climbed down from the cockpit and stretched her tight muscles, watching as her flight crew went through the routine of checking the aircraft and preparing it for the return trip. The crew chief, Sergeant First Class Samantha Helwig, began coordinating with the ground personnel to unload the supplies and mailbags that she carried in her cargo bay, while a fuel truck lumbered toward them. Nearby, the other two helicopters were undergoing similar activity.

A soldier jogged toward her across the tarmac, a clipboard beneath his arm. Jenna returned his smart salute.

"Hey, Corporal Garrett." She smiled, recognizing the man from her previous visits. "Who do we have the privilege of transporting today?"

The soldier consulted his clipboard. "A five-man unit for you, and two VIPs for Captain McLaughlin."

"Right," she replied, and glanced in the direction of the other Black Hawk, where she could see the pilot inspecting his aircraft. She wouldn't speculate on the reasons why McLaughlin always got the VIPs. Her job was to transport personnel. End of story. Her helicopter was large enough to accommodate her four-person crew and seven fully equipped troops, so the five-man team put her almost at full capacity.

Turning away, she began a visual inspection of her own helicopter, looking for any structural damage or weaknesses in the aircraft. She'd been flying with Warrant Officer Costanza for so long now that she no longer thought about the fact that they were the only all-female crew in her battalion. Even her door gunner and her crew chief were women. They all had hundreds of flying hours under their belts, and each took their job seriously. Given a choice, Jenna knew she would choose these women to crew her aircraft over any of the guys in her battalion.

"Just another day at the office," Laura said brightly, climbing onto the fuselage to inspect the rotor shaft. She slanted Jenna a small smile, reading the direction of her thoughts. "For what it's worth, I'm sure the VIPs have no clue about who's piloting which helicopter. It's not personal."

Jenna shrugged. "It doesn't matter. I'm here to do a job, not suck up to some general who happens to be riding in my jump seat." She cast another dark look across the tarmac to where Captain Kevin "Mongo" McLaughlin was checking out his tail rotor. "But I know he's going to gloat over this later, and that just bugs me."

Laura was only half listening. Her attention was fixated on the other side of the tarmac, where a group of five soldiers were making their way toward the helicopter. Even as Jenna bent to look through the open cabin doors for a better view, Laura scrambled swiftly down.

"Forget Mongo and his gloating," she hissed, pretending to fiddle with the sliding door of the cabin while her dark gaze remained riveted on the men. "Check these guys out!"

Jenna frowned. Heat shimmered over the asphalt, distorting their figures as they strode closer, and for a moment she was reminded of the iconic Hollywood scene from the blockbuster movie *Armageddon,* when five heroic astronauts made their way in slow motion across the flight line on a mission to save the world. Only, instead of orange space suits, these guys wore desert camouflage and carried army-issued duffel bags. But beneath the rim of their helmets, their sunburned faces sported several weeks' worth of beard, and each wore the same don't-fuck-with-me expression.

"Another special ops team," mused Jenna. In the two months of her deployment, she and Laura had transported dozens of special ops commandos from one location to another. While Jenna knew the likelihood of running into Chase Rawlins was slim, her heart did a small flip of anticipation each time one of them climbed aboard her helicopter. "Looks like they've been outside the wire for a while."

"Oh, yeah," murmured Laura in an appreciative tone. "Looks like they could use some serious R and R, and I know just the person to give it to them. Come to Mama, boys."

Jenna laughed softly, no longer shocked by anything that Laura said. She knew the other woman was mostly talk and almost no action.

As the men drew closer, conversing with each other in low tones, Jenna's eyes narrowed. There was something about the guy on the far right. He was tall and lean, and walked with an easy, loose-limbed grace that reminded her of—

"Holy crap!"

Laura's gaze flashed between her and the group of men, and back again. "What? You know one of them?"

Quickly, before the group got any closer, Jenna spun out of sight and pressed her back against the side of the helicopter, adrenaline surging hot and hard through her veins.

"Don't let him see me," she whispered fiercely.

"Who?" Laura craned her head so that she was looking through the open doors of the cabin, just as the first man climbed up through the opposite door and into the helicopter. She straightened abruptly and snapped out a salute. "Afternoon, sir," she said in a no-nonsense military tone. "I'm Warrant Officer Costanza, your copilot. As soon as we're refueled, we'll depart."

Jenna heard the low rumble of a reply, and then Laura stepped smartly away from the door and made her way toward the front of the helicopter, dragging Jenna with her. "Is that who I think it is?" she hissed, incredulous. "Is it the guy from Shooters?"

"Yes. No! I don't know! I can't be sure." Jenna's heart was slamming so hard in her chest that she was sure Laura must hear it. "I didn't exactly stop to read his name tag! *God.*"

But when she pressed her fingers against her closed eyes, she could see him clearly and knew that she hadn't been mistaken. And what were the freaking chances that she would run into Major Chase Rawlins out here, a gazillion miles from Fort Bragg, in the middle of freaking no-man's land? There was no doubt in her mind that it was him. Even with half his face covered in scruff, his eyes hidden behind a pair of dark sunglasses, she'd recognize him.

She'd thought of him more often than she'd care to admit—even to herself—during the past two months. The one night she'd spent with him was as fresh in her mind as if it had been only yesterday. What would he do when he saw her? Would he even recognize her? Did he ever think of her?

"Breathe."

Jenna opened her eyes to see Laura watching her closely. She dragged in a deep breath. Her glance flicked to the open door of the cabin, where she could hear the men getting settled.

"I'm okay," she muttered, pushing the other woman aside. "It just took me by surprise, that's all. Some co-incidence, huh?"

Laura arched one slim eyebrow. "I don't believe in coincidences. This was bound to happen."

"How do you figure?"

Laura gestured toward the surrounding mountains. "Hello! We're in Taliban country. He's Special Ops, which means his main mission is hunting the bad guys, and where do you think they're hiding?"

Jenna gave her a tolerant look. "I understand, but—"

"We fly to damn near every U.S. installation in Afghanistan. We transport personnel, including special ops teams." Laura's voice was firm with conviction. "It was only a matter of time before you ran into him."

Jenna groaned and scrubbed a hand over her face. "But what do I say to him? How do I act? He couldn't wait to get rid of me that night. What if he doesn't even remember me?"

"Trust me," Laura said drily, "he'll remember you."

"Ma'am?"

Both women turned to see Corporal Garrett rounding the nose of the helicopter. "You're fully loaded and refueled."

Jenna forced herself to nod, but it was an effort to act normal when every cell in her body screamed with awareness of the man who had rocked her world just two months ago and then vanished from her life.

"Thank you," she replied, and turned to Laura. "Let's do this."

She climbed into the cockpit and greeted the hard-eyed men who sat in the cabin, hoping her voice didn't betray the fact that she was a bundle of nerves.

"Welcome aboard, gentlemen. I'm Captain Larson and your copilot today is Chief Warrant Officer Costanza. We'll be departing shortly. Our ETA at Kabul Air Base is approximately seventeen hundred hours." Her gaze touched briefly on each man in turn and then lingered on Chase. "Sit back and enjoy the flight."

He stared back at her impassively, and then gave her a brief nod before turning to say something to the man on his left. They might have been complete strangers, for all the notice he took of her. Jenna watched him for another few seconds, taking in the familiar thrust of his shoulders, the strong jaw beneath the shadow of his beard and the chiseled cheekbones. The only thing missing was the lazy smile and devilish glint in his eyes that had first attracted her to him.

As if sensing her scrutiny, he turned his attention back to her and raised one eyebrow in silent query. But his light green eyes were remote, and Jenna could read nothing in their cool depths except polite expectation.

So that was how it was going to be.

Jenna felt her face go hot in a swift, physical reaction to his dismissal. Was he deliberately pretending not to know her in order to spare her feelings? Or did he think they needed to keep their prior relationship a secret? She gave Chase one last, meaningful look before she turned her back on him and jammed her helmet onto her head.

Laura leaned toward her over the center controls,

pretending to adjust one of the gauges. "Hey," she said in a low voice as Jenna powered up the rotors, "you okay?"

"Fine," she breathed. "It's probably better this way. I mean, even if he did remember me and was interested in getting together again, it's not like we'd have the chance."

She slid a swift glance over her shoulder at Chase, sharp regret slicing through her. He had tipped his head back and closed his eyes, and Jenna could see the lines of fatigue on his face. Even with his eyes shut, the guy was mouthwatering.

It just wasn't fair.

Her flight plan included dropping him and his team off at Kabul Air Base, and then spending the night in a Barracks hut with Laura and the rest of her crew. In the morning, she would return to her duty station at Kandahar Air Base, three hundred miles to the south. The chances of their paths crossing even once had been slim, but the likelihood that they would cross a second time was about one in a hundred thousand, and that was being optimistic.

Even so, for the entire return flight to Kabul Air Base, Jenna was acutely conscious of the man who sat less than four feet behind her, the same man that she hadn't been able to stop thinking about since that night by Pope airfield. Despite the fact that he'd claimed not to have a problem with her being a pilot, his entire manner had changed after she'd told him what she did for a living.

Typical.

She shouldn't feel so disappointed, but she'd really hoped he might be different. He'd driven her back to the officer's barracks at Fort Bragg and had even kissed her sweetly before he'd stepped away from her.

"Maybe we'll run into each other again someday," he'd said, and his expression had been brooding. "If we do, I hope you won't think badly of me."

She had lain awake for most of that night, replaying the events of the evening over and over in her mind and wondering what he had meant by his parting words. Did he think she would want more than just one night together, or that she believed he had misled her somehow? Did he think she would turn into one of those overly emotional women who felt that one night of sex—albeit incredible sex—entitled her to a happy-ever-after?

As they flew south, away from the Hindu Kush mountains and toward Kabul Air Base, it took all of Jenna's training to concentrate on doing her job and not continually glance back at Chase. She was shocked by how much she wanted to reconnect with him. For one, brief instant, she'd considered the possibility that he really didn't remember her, but had just as quickly rejected the idea. There was no way he had forgotten her, not when the memory of that night was still so vivid for her. Something just didn't make sense. The male appreciation that she'd come to expect whenever he looked at her had been completely absent in his eyes. Okay, so maybe her flight suit and helmet weren't exactly sexy, and maybe he had other things on his mind, considering he'd just returned from a mission, but she'd expected to at least see a spark of recognition.

There had been nothing.

Logically, she knew he was sending her a clear message, but the irrational part of her—the part that apparently couldn't stop thinking about him—didn't want to listen. As they flew south, Jenna made up her mind; she was going to confront Chase, if only to let him know that she didn't think badly of him, as he'd once suggested she might. She would be as cool and detached as he was, but she knew that if he gave any indication that he might be interested in a repeat performance, she would consider it.

It wouldn't mean anything. She was just feeling physically deprived because she hadn't been with anyone since her night with Chase. What she was feeling was a natural physical response to a gorgeous guy, and whatever they had was definitely physical. There was absolutely no way she was in any danger of falling for the guy.

None. Whatsoever.

5

As they drew closer to Kabul Air Base, it became clear to Jenna that her piloting skills were going to be tested. A sandstorm had engulfed the region, forcing her to rely solely on her instrumentation when visibility became so poor that she could no longer make out any landmarks. She knew from experience that landing in a sandstorm would produce a dense cloud that could easily disorient or blind a pilot. Attempting to land in brownout conditions was a major cause of lateral rollovers and ground collisions. She would essentially be flying a controlled crash into the ground with no outside reference.

"Brownout landing procedures initiated," Jenna said, flipping a gauge to turn on a small liquid-crystal display that charted velocity vector, acceleration cures, radar altimeter height and vertical speed. Laura called out the ground speed and drift, airspeed, altitude, wind speed and direction on the cockpit hover display.

According to the instrumentation, they were directly above the designated landing spot, although Jenna could see absolutely nothing through the windshield or floor canopy of the helicopter. Thick, brown dust swirled around them, made even worse by the wash of the rotor blades.

"Hover stabilization system activated," Jenna said, adjusting the hover hold function in the tilt rotor flight controls.

"Three feet to ground," Laura confirmed, watching the hover display. "Two feet. One."

They came to rest with hardly a bump, and both Jenna and Laura initiated routine shutdown procedures.

"Welcome to Kabul Air Base," Jenna said through her intercom. "Enjoy your stay, and as always, thank you for flying with the U.S. Army. We know you have no other options, but we still appreciate your business."

Unlike her previous passengers, she didn't get any chuckles from this group. As the rotor blades whirred to a stop, she could just make out the nearby hangar through the swirling clouds of dust. Pulling a handkerchief out of her pocket and a pair of goggles from her flight bag, she removed her helmet and wrapped the cloth around her face, pulling the goggles into place.

"I hate this shit," Laura said, doing the same. "No matter how long I stand under a shower, it feels like I never get rid of all the sand."

Jenna could sympathize. Even now, as her crew chief slid the cabin doors open, hot air gusted in, bringing the choking dust with it. In a matter of seconds, the entire interior of the chopper was covered in a fine coating of powdery silt. It would take her and the crew forever to get it clean again. She twisted in her seat and watched as the team of special operators made their way from the helicopter. Like herself and Laura, they had also donned goggles and scarves over their faces, but she had no trouble spotting Chase. She would recognize his build anywhere.

"Nice landing, Captain," Laura said, her voice muffled by her kerchief.

"Couldn't have done it without you, Chief," Jenna replied, watching Chase as he strode away and was swallowed up in the swirling dust. Grabbing her flight bag, she opened the door and prepared to climb down. "Can you finish the paperwork? There's something I have to do."

"No problem."

But Jenna could see the speculation in the other woman's eyes as she jumped lightly down from the cockpit and began jogging toward the hangar, holding the handkerchief in place with one hand over her mouth and nose. Inside the hangar, she could see the five-man team just ahead, and she yanked her kerchief away from her face.

"Major Rawlins!"

He turned and looked back at her, pushing his goggles up to his forehead. Jenna slowed to a walk, watching as he said something to the other men and indicated they should go ahead without him. He waited, hefting his duffel bag a little higher on his shoulder. She walked toward him, her heart beginning to hammer in a way that had nothing to do with her brief sprint across the tarmac.

His sunburned face was covered in dust, making his light green eyes all the more startling. "That was some nice flying, Captain," he said as she came to a stop in front of him. "Is there something I can help you with?"

His tone was so cool and polite that for a brief instant Jenna couldn't find her voice. She wondered if she wasn't making a huge mistake. She had hoped that, once they were alone, he would drop the pretense of not knowing her, but apparently he wasn't going to give her the satisfaction. She would have to brazen it out.

"I just wanted to say hi, and let you know that I don't think badly of you. Just the opposite, in fact."

His eyes narrowed and he looked at her uncertainly. "Okay...thanks."

Jenna waited for him to drop the act, but after an awkward moment where the silence stretched between them, she gave him a bright smile. "Well, that's pretty much what I wanted to say. I'm spending the night here, so if you want to...you know...get together, just say the word. I'm sure we could find somewhere private."

He cocked his head, and one corner of his mouth tilted in a ghost of the smile she found so attractive. When he spoke, his voice sounded slightly strangled. "Are you propositioning me?"

Jenna felt her own smile falter. "Um, yes, actually. I believe I am."

He laughed softly and scratched the bridge of his nose. "Wow. I don't know what to say."

Jenna felt her irritation rising. "How about 'Jeez, that sounds great. I'd love to'?"

He shifted his weight, and his gaze traveled slowly over her. "Listen, you're a beautiful woman—don't get me wrong—and I may kick myself in the ass later for saying this, but I'm going to have to pass on your offer."

Jenna felt her mouth open in dismay before she snapped it closed.

"But I am flattered," he said, no doubt in an effort to reassure her. "It's just that I don't mix business with pleasure."

He was parroting her own words back to her, the very words she had said to him when she'd tried to explain why she avoided getting involved with guys in uniform.

She drew in a deep breath and felt a burning tide of humiliation color her face. "Fine," she finally said, trying to sound nonchalant. Businesslike. "I completely understand. But you can't blame a girl for trying, right? Have a good evening, Major."

She heard him curse softly under his breath, but before he could say anything else to her, she spun on her heel and strode away from him. She walked blindly, her pulse pounding hotly in her ears, willing herself not to do something really idiotic like cry. She was so not going to cry. But as she made her way toward the B-Huts where she would spend the night, she could feel the hot sting of tears and was grateful for the swirling dust that concealed her weakness.

She'd been grounded.

For at least two days, maybe more, until the dust storm that was raging through the region had passed. She had no business flying in these conditions, but there was no way Jenna wanted to remain at Kabul, knowing *he* was somewhere on the base.

"Where are you going?" From the narrow bed next to her own, Laura lifted the pillow she had bunched over her head and peered at her watch. "It's barely five o'clock in the morning."

"I've already been over to the flight line," Jenna said, keeping her voice low in consideration of the other two women who were trying to sleep in the small hut. "We've been grounded for at least two days due to the sandstorm."

"Oh, thank God," Laura muttered, and dropped her

head back down, her fists curling into the pillow and arranging it around her ears. "I can finally sleep late."

"I'm going over to the gym," Jenna said in a whisper, sitting on the edge of her bed as she scooped her hair into a ponytail. "Do you mind watching my weapon? I'll be back in a few hours."

The only response was the sound of light snoring.

Jenna envied the other woman. Sleep had eluded her, and she'd spent most of the night lying awake in bed, thinking about Chase Rawlins and the fact that he had rejected her. In fact, he'd turned her down flat.

If she didn't know better, she'd think he really didn't remember their encounter, but she gave him more credit than that. He knew she was a helicopter pilot, and how many female Black Hawk pilots were there? Jenna could count them on both hands. There was no way he wouldn't remember that detail, since it had pretty much ruined their night.

Wrapping her kerchief over her face, she walked across the dark compound to the gym, which was housed in an enormous, rounded tent stretched over accordion-like metal supports. Dust still swirled across the base, and by the time she reached the gym, her eyes felt gritty, and she spent five minutes shaking the powdery sand from her hair and clothes. It was early enough that she had the place almost entirely to herself, with just two men lifting free weights at the far end of the tent. She chose an elliptical machine at the opposite end to begin her workout.

Within fifteen minutes, she had established a rhythm that got her heart rate up and caused a light sweat to break out on her skin. She was so caught up in her own thoughts that she didn't immediately notice the group of men who came in and made their way toward the weight equipment, until one of them dropped a weight with an enormous clang. Startled, she looked over at them and nearly lost her smooth stride.

Two men stood flexing free weights, while another used the lateral pull-down weights. But her attention was riveted on the man who lay on the weight bench, his feet planted firmly on the floor as he lifted a weight in each hand and brought them together over his chest. Every muscle in his impressive arms and across his shoulders bulged with effort, and beneath the T-shirt, she could see his pecs and abdominal muscles contract with each repetition.

Chase.

As if sensing her scrutiny, he turned his head and their gazes locked. For just an instant, his expression registered utter shock, and he nearly dropped the weights. Jenna dragged her attention back to the elliptical machine and turned the power off, her heart racing. She couldn't face Chase right now. She'd spent the entire night tossing and turning because of him, and she felt tired and achy and vulnerable. There was no way she'd be able to act as if she didn't care.

As if she didn't still want him.

Snatching her towel up, she left the workout area, pausing only long enough to wind the towel around her face before she walked swiftly toward the exit and into the swirling dust storm. Her legs felt rubbery and weak, both from the exercise and in reaction to seeing Chase. She had gone less than fifty feet when she heard his voice.

"Jenna!"

Putting her head down, she quickened her pace, determined to ignore him. She wouldn't stop. If she stopped, she'd be toast. She couldn't even begin to identify the whirlwind of feelings that consumed her, but she knew that, in her current state, she wouldn't stand a chance against his potent charm.

"Damn it to hell, Jenna, would you hold up?"

She should have known that he wouldn't let her just walk away. Blowing out a hard breath, she stopped and turned to face him as he jogged to catch up with her. Unlike her, he wore no protection against the blowing dust, and used one hand to shield his mouth and nose. He glanced around and then grabbed her by the arm, pulling her with him to a nearby structure. Opening the door, he thrust her inside and followed her, shutting out the storm. One small, dirty window allowed weak light to penetrate the darkness and Jenna saw they were in a storage unit filled with excess fitness equipment. Beside her, Chase was swiping the sand from his hair and face, sending up small clouds of powdery dust.

"What the hell are you doing here?" he demanded, his eyes raking over her.

"Working out," she replied coolly, hoping the indistinct light hid the fact that she was trembling.

There was something different about him, and it took her a couple of seconds to realize that he had shaved the scruff of beard from his jaw. He shook his head as if in disbelief.

"I thought I was seeing things," he said, sounding incredulous. "Jesus, I haven't been able to stop thinking about you, and— Come here."

Before Jenna could react, he dragged her up against his hard chest, his hands sliding around her stiff body as he lowered his head and covered her mouth with his own. For one long, blissful moment, Jenna was too shocked to protest. The only thing in the world was Chase and the hot, insistent pressure of his lips against hers. In the next instant, sanity returned and she struggled to break free from his embrace. He released her immediately.

"Sorry," he said. His voice was gruff, but the roguish grin that she loved was back. "I just had to do that."

Jenna struggled to recall why she had pulled away. When it looked as if he might actually reach for her again, she put her hands up to forestall him.

"Whoa. Stop."

"What's going on?" He spread his arms out, but that only drew her attention to his amazing biceps and shoulders. Her mouth began to water.

"I don't know what game you're playing," she finally managed, dragging her gaze upward to his face, "but I am not going to be your dirty little secret. So if you think you can pretend not to know me in front of your guys, and then go all sweet on me when we're alone, you are so out of luck."

She saw the puzzlement in his eyes. "What are you talking about? If you hadn't hightailed it out of the gym so fast, I would have come over to you and demonstrated to anyone who cared to watch just how well I *do* know you. As it is, the guys think I've lost my mind, chasing you outside in this shit." He scrubbed a hand over his hair, sending renewed puffs of dust into the air. "Jesus. For a moment there, I thought I was hallucinating. I still can't get my head around it. When did you get here?"

Jenna narrowed her eyes and studied him. "Don't screw with me, Chase. You know damn well when I got here."

As she watched, his face altered and his expression grew shuttered. When he spoke, his voice was cold. "What did you just call me?"

Jenna frowned. "Chase."

She gave an audible gasp of surprise when he grabbed her by the upper arms and pulled her so close that their faces were mere inches apart and she could feel the warmth of his breath fanning her face.

"What's my name?" he growled.

"What?"

"Tell me my name," he repeated in a hard tone, his fingers biting into her shoulders.

"Chase Rawlins."

"When did we first meet?"

Jenna shook her head, not understanding. "I don't—"

"Answer the damned question, Jenna!" His voice was so tight with controlled fury that Jenna felt a frisson of fear tiptoe its way up her spine.

"Technically, we met that night at Shooters, when you drove me out to the airfield. But I ran into you at the supermarket before that."

He relaxed fractionally, but didn't release her. "Apart from that night by the airfield, you've never been with me? Never kissed me or had sex with me?"

"What?" She pushed weakly against his chest. "You know I haven't!"

He gave her a slight shake. "You called me Rawlins that night at the club. How did you know my name?"

Jenna stared at him, bewildered by his interrogation. Maybe he'd suffered a head injury and had some kind of short-term memory loss. Why else would he be acting so strangely?

"My roommate told me," she explained carefully. "She saw me watching you at the club that night and said you were special ops. She knew your name. Don't you remember that night?"

His eyes grew hot, and she knew that he remembered everything. Then he swore under his breath and released her, dragging his hands over his face before he pinned her with a calculating look. "Come with me. There's something I need to show you."

Before she could protest, he wrapped her towel around her face and opened the door, pulling her out into the storm. She stumbled to keep up with him as he practically dragged her across the base, seemingly oblivious to the choking dust that whipped around them. She knew he was agitated, since he hadn't bothered to cover his own face. The blowing sand and grit made it impossible for her to speak, and nearly impossible to see where they were going.

He finally pulled her to a stop in front of a containerized housing unit, or CHU, which was nothing more than a shipping container that had been prefabricated into living quarters. An air conditioner was mounted into the wall beside the door, and hummed noisily. Chase hammered on the door with his fist until finally it was yanked open. Jenna found herself pulled into a tiny living area sparsely furnished with a desk and a couple of chairs.

Unwinding the towel from her head, she used it to wipe the grit from her eyes before she turned to face Chase. A second man stood by the door, wearing nothing but a pair of shorts, and it was clear they had roused him from sleep. Jenna blinked, convinced that the dust was making her see double. Stunned, she stared at the man, taking in the scruffy beard and the hard eyes that watched her warily. Her gaze flicked to Chase, who stood with his arms crossed over his chest, waiting.

"What the hell...?" Jenna was only vaguely aware that she had uttered the words aloud. Except for the beard, the two men were identical in every respect.

"Jenna, I'd like you to meet my brother, *Chase* Rawlins," said the man who had kissed her just moments before. "My *twin* brother, Chase. *He's* special ops."

Jenna felt her mouth fall open as she gaped first at the real Chase, who had the grace to give her a sheepish grin, and then at... Who *was* the man she'd just kissed, and hadn't been able to stop thinking about?

"So if you're Chase," she said weakly, before switching her gaze to the other man, "who are *you?*"

"I'm Major *Chance* Rawlins, call sign 'T-Rex.' Apache helicopter pilot and the guy you...met at Shooters. Pleased to meet you."

Jenna didn't miss the hesitation in his words. Not only was he the guy she'd met at Shooters, he was the guy she'd screwed blind mere hours later. A guy she'd believed to be a special ops soldier, when in fact he was a helicopter pilot.

A pilot.

"Oh, my God," she breathed with dawning horror.

She'd broken her own number-one rule: she'd slept with a pilot! Worse, after they'd had sex, she'd talked trash about male pilots and their inability to have any kind of meaningful relationship. No wonder he'd ended their evening so abruptly.

"I, um, I need some air," she finally said, and fled.

6

CHASE STEPPED ASIDE AS Jenna wrenched the door open and bolted into the swirling sandstorm.

"Jenna, wait!" Chance tried to sprint after her, but found his way blocked by a muscular arm.

"Let her go, bro," Chase said quietly. "She needs some time."

"It's a goddamned duststorm," Chance bit out. "I am not letting her lose her way out there."

"She's not stupid. She'll be fine."

Chance had never felt such impotent anger, and with a savage curse, he kicked at the open door, causing it to slam back on its hinges. "Goddamn it!"

"So that's her, huh?" Chase mused, pulling the door closed. He turned to a coffeemaker on the shelf and began measuring out coffee and water. "The mystery lady from Shooters. The reason you missed my send-off party. I can see why you like her, although I have to say she's a far cry from your usual type. Did I mention that I hitched a ride with her from Kalagush yesterday? She seemed interested in me when I climbed into the chopper, but I didn't expect her to hit on me after we landed."

Chance felt his chest tighten in an unexpected surge of jealousy. "She hit on you? Jesus, if you—"

"Relax," his brother said with a rare grin. "Nothing happened. I was too beat to take her up on the offer."

"Lucky for you," Chance muttered. "I'd hate to have to kick my own brother's ass."

"Ha," Chase scoffed good-naturedly. "You and whose army? If it makes you feel any better, she only did it because she thought I was you."

"Yeah, well, I wish you'd told me about it last night. I might have put two and two together and realized she was here."

Chase arched an eyebrow. "If I took the time to tell you about every chick who hits on me—"

"it'd be the shortest conversation in history," Chance interrupted, aiming a friendly punch at his brother's arm.

"Still, what are the chances, huh? It's pretty hilarious when you think about it."

Chance disagreed. While he and his brother had played their fair share of jokes on friends and teachers when they were kids, they'd drawn the line at switching identities to fool the opposite sex. Mostly because Chance had been unwilling to leave his girlfriend alone with his brother, even for a few minutes.

Although the two of them looked identical, there had always been something about Chase that drew girls to him like moths to a flame. He didn't even need to do anything and girls hovered in his airspace, hoping to attract his attention. And it just seemed to annoy him. But right now, Chance didn't find anything remotely funny about the fact that Jenna had actually hit on Chase. In fact, for the first time he could recall, he found himself feeling resentful toward his twin, and wishing that they weren't located on the same base, even if it was just for a couple of days.

Chance flew with the 82nd Aviation Regiment, or the Wolf Pack, the army's only airborne attack helicopter battalion. He'd arrived at Kabul Air Base a month earlier and had spent the past four weeks supporting ground troops. He knew that Chase and his special ops team had been sent to a forward operating base in northern Afghanistan, but his brother's exact location had not been disclosed.

He'd been pleasantly surprised when Chase had knocked on the door of his housing unit last night to let him know he was at Kabul for a couple of days. This was Chance's fourth deployment, and God only knew how many times Chase had been over here. Too many to count. He'd been one of the first special ops teams to put boots on the ground after the invasion, and Chance suspected his brother would continue to conduct operations long after the majority of troops were sent home.

Their deployments had overlapped before, but it was rare that they were both located on the same base at the same time. Kabul Air Base was so large, however, that Chance found himself running into people he'd served with years earlier and had never expected to see again. There was a saying that if you stayed at Kabul long enough, eventually you'd meet every soldier who served in the army.

Not knowing how long he might be at Kabul, Chase had gone straight to Chance's quarters and the two brothers had stayed up late into the night, catching up on each other's lives over the past two months. Chance had admitted that he'd missed his brother's going-away party because he'd met a woman, but he hadn't given Chase any details. It didn't seem likely that the relationship would develop into anything meaningful. In fact, considering the things Jenna had said that night, the likelihood she would even speak to him again was about nil.

"Well," Chase said when Chance was silent, "it isn't the first time you've been mistaken for me." He poured each of them a steaming mug of coffee.

"You've got it backward," Chance retorted. "You said it yourself. The only reason she spoke to you is because she mistook *you* for *me*."

"Did you know she was going to be here at Kabul?"

"Of course not. We were only together that one night and we didn't exactly spend time talking about future deployments," Chance added sourly. "In fact, I didn't even know she was active duty until after we'd—" He broke off and stared moodily out of the window at the blowing sand.

Chase peered at his brother over the rim of his mug. "She looked seriously pissed off."

Chance shrugged. "Apparently, she has a thing about sleeping with pilots."

His brother raised his eyebrows. "As in…she likes to sleep with them?"

"Ah, no," Chance said drily. "As in…she'd rather suffer all the scourges of hell than sleep with even one pilot."

To Chance's chagrin, his brother began to laugh. "So let me get this straight," Chase said, when he could finally speak again. "She slept with you, thinking you were *me*."

"No. She slept with me thinking I was special ops," Chance clarified.

"Right. So you knew she had a thing about pilots, and yet you still did her? Why didn't you tell her right then that you were one?"

"I had no idea how she felt about pilots, and by the time she let me know, the deed was done. I didn't see any point in making her feel bad about it." Not when she'd felt so good in his arms. He rubbed the back of his neck. "Besides, I didn't think we'd ever see each other again."

"But you'd hoped."

Yeah, he had hoped. Despite the fact that she'd delivered a serious blow to his self-esteem with her remarks about pilots, once he'd gotten over his ego, he'd gone straight to Fort Bragg where her battalion was headquartered, intending to tell her the truth about himself. He hadn't been able to stop thinking about her. He'd wanted an opportunity to prove to her that he wasn't like the guys she worked with.

But he'd discovered that her entire unit had gone wheels up to Afghanistan, and would be stationed at Kandahar Air Base for the next six months. When his own unit had geared up for deployment a month later, he'd hoped like hell they would be sent to Kandahar, but they'd been assigned to Kabul, easily three hundred miles to the north.

"So now she knows the truth," Chase said, sipping his coffee and watching Chance with a contemplative look. "What are you going to do about it?"

"What do you think?" Chance set his mug down on the shelf and stood, grabbing a pair of goggles and a scarf from a hook near the door. "I'll return these."

"Yeah, yeah. Better hurry, or the storm will be over and she'll be gone."

CHANCE KNEW WHERE the itinerant pilots were housed, but when he finally found the housing area for the female crew members and pounded on the door, it wasn't Jenna who answered.

"This better be an emergency," grumbled a small, dark-haired woman with a purple satin eye mask pushed up onto her forehead. She held a handkerchief over her mouth and stood well back from the doorway as she peered through the swirling dust at Chance. Then her eyes widened and she dropped the cloth away from her face. She looked panicked as she snatched the eye mask from her head and made an attempt to stand at attention. "Sir! Good morning, sir!"

"At ease, Soldier."

She relaxed fractionally. "What are you doing here? Sir."

"I'm looking for Jenna. Is she here?"

"No, she went over to the gym about an hour ago."

Anxiety knifed its way through his gut. She should have been back to her quarters by now. Kabul Air Base was enormous. It would be all too easy to get disoriented or lost, especially with the reduced visibility. Frustrated and concerned, he shielded his eyes and scanned the surrounding area, as if he could will her into sight.

"Is she familiar with the base?" he asked.

The woman shrugged. "As much as any other itinerant pilot, I guess." She opened the door wider and stepped back. "You'd better come in, or we're both going to die of asphyxiation."

Chance hesitated, then stepped inside the structure, resisting the urge to shake the sand out of his hair. There were rules against males entering a female's living quarters, but he told himself this was a unique situation. Glancing around, he saw the B-Hut was out-fitted with four small sleeping quarters, but the woman who had answered the door was the only occupant. She wore a pair of baggy sweatpants and an army T-shirt, and now she appraised him with open curiosity.

"We've been to Kabul before," she said, planting her hands on her hips. "Which begs the question…what the hell are *you* doing here?"

Chance sharpened his gaze on her, a suspicion form-ing in his mind. "Have we met?"

She tossed the eye mask and kerchief onto a nearby chair and smiled at him. "No, but I remember you from the club back home." She extended her hand. "Warrant Officer Laura Costanza. I'm Captain Larson's copilot."

Chance shook her hand. "Major Chance Rawlins… I'm a pilot with the 82nd Aviation Regiment."

He watched with grim satisfaction as her smile faded. "You're a Wolf Pack pilot?" she asked, refer-ring to the battalion's call sign. "But I thought… I was told you were special forces."

"That would be my twin brother, Chase." He cocked his head. "Why? Is there a problem?"

Laura looked helplessly at him. "She's sworn off pilots."

"Yeah, I got that memo. Do you know why?"

"Because you're all a bunch of self—"

"Yeah, I got that memo, too," he interrupted tersely. "Was she involved with a pilot? Someone who hurt her?"

"No, not since I've known her. The only other pilot in her life is her dad, and he's a freaking hero."

Chance frowned. "Who's her father?"

"Captain Erik Larson, Medal of Honor recipient."

Chance gaped at her. "*The* Erik Larson? The Vietnam pilot?"

Anyone who flew a military helicopter knew about Erik Larson, and how he successfully completed fifteen missions into enemy territory to airlift injured soldiers out of war zones that were deemed too dangerous for medevac choppers. The guy wasn't just a hero; he was a legend.

"The same," Laura confirmed. "After the war was over, he left the army and started his own helicopter sightseeing business. From what I hear, he taught Jenna everything he knew about flying."

"Does Jenna ever talk about him?"

Laura shook her head and mouthed the word *nope.* "That subject is off-limits."

Which explained a lot.

"Okay, thanks," he said. "Look, where would Jenna go if she was upset?"

Laura shrugged. "Somewhere private, where nobody would bug her, I guess."

And just like that, Chance knew where she was.

"Thanks," he said, and bolted back into the swirling dust. He made his way across the base to the flight line. There were very few people out at this early hour, especially with the sandstorm. Aside from several security details, Chance saw only a couple of other soldiers making their way toward the dining facility.

He reached the hangar closest to the helipad and ducked inside. An Apache helicopter sat in the middle of the open space and two mechanics were working on the engine. They glanced up as Chance walked through, noting his PT clothing, but they didn't challenge him.

"Which pad are the Black Hawks parked on?" he asked. The dust was so thick that he could barely see

his own hand in front of his face, never mind a Black
Hawk helicopter several hundred yards away.

One of the mechanics gestured toward the right.
"A couple of them are over there. But all birds are
grounded until this shit clears up. Can I help you with
something?"

"No, thanks." Chance pulled his military ID free
from his pocket and flashed it toward them. "I'm looking for a female pilot who may have come through here
a little while ago."

The two men exchanged a meaningful look. "Yeah…
she's over in tail number Romeo-Echo-Hotel-five-six-
one."

Muttering his thanks, Chance left the hangar and
made his way over to the helipad. As he got closer, he
could just make out the dark, looming shape of several helicopters, and paused to read their tail numbers.
REH561 was the third chopper on the pad, and the one
farthest from the hangar. Without pausing to reconsider
his actions, he slid the cabin door open and climbed
inside, pulling the door tightly closed against a gust of
swirling sand and grit.

"What are *you* doing here?" asked a feminine voice,
clearly laced with hostility.

Relief swamped him. Removing his goggles, Chance
glanced around the small compartment until he saw
Jenna at the rear of the cabin. She sat slumped in one of
the troop seats. Keeping his head low, he picked his way
carefully around the equipment and wiring on the floor
and lowered himself into the seat next to hers. This
dust-covered, despondent version of Jenna seemed so
starkly different from the woman who had boldly straddled his Harley that for a moment he was taken aback.
He wanted to touch her so bad, to drag her across his

lap and just hold her. Instead, he linked his fingers together between his knees and angled his head to look at her.

"Hey," he said softly, bumping his shoulder against hers. "You okay?"

She pulled away and refused to look at him, focusing instead on her hands. "I was. Until you showed up. Why are you here? To gloat?"

"Why would i gloat?"

She turned her head to give him a tolerant look, and he could see the misery in her hazel eyes. "Why is your call sign T-Rex?"

"What?" Chance was unprepared for the sudden change in subject. Call signs were the nicknames given to aviation pilots and crew members. "I guess because as an Apache pilot, I'm one of the biggest, baddest predators out there. And because I'm from Texas and T-Rex sort of sounds like a shortened version of Texas. Why?"

"Do you know what my call sign is?" she finally asked.

Chance shook his head. "I have no idea."

"Goalie."

"Ah. As in everyone tries to hit on the goalie?" He'd not only hit on her, he'd scored. Big-time.

"If the guys in my battalion ever find out…"

Chance knew this was his cue to assure her that he'd never tell anyone about that night, and promise her it would never happen again. But the words stuck in his throat. There was no way he'd utter them, because they weren't true, and if he had anything to say about it, they'd be doing the same thing again soon and as often as possible after that.

"I didn't take you for the type to feel sorry for yourself," he said casually, studying the backs of his hands.

"I'm not feeling sorry for myself," she retorted with indignation.

"Good," he replied, his voice sounding rougher than he intended. "Because I'm not sorry about that night, and I'm not going to apologize for what happened between us. I had no freaking clue you were a pilot, or that you had some dumb-ass rule about not hooking up with other pilots." He pinned her with a hard glare. "Not that it would have made a difference."

She made a snorting sound that ended on a groan of self-loathing. "If this ever gets out—"

"What?" he demanded, spreading his hands. He sympathized with her, he really did, but he was quickly losing his patience. "What's the worst that would happen? People would realize that you're human after all?"

"You're a guy. It's different for you. You wouldn't understand."

"Try me." When she remained quiet, he tipped his head back and blew out a hard breath. "Okay, you know what? The next time you decide to sleep with a stranger, do yourself a favor and at least get the guy's name, rank and social-security number, okay?"

He was deliberately callous in an attempt to piss her off, because anger would be a whole lot easier to deal with than self-pity. If she started to cry, he'd be toast. To his surprise, she slanted him an amused glance.

"I thought I had," she said. "Well, except for the social-security number. What are the chances that twin brothers would be assigned to the same base?"

Chance shrugged, relieved by her response. "I have a little more leeway about where I want to be assigned than Chase does. His unit is based permanently out of Fort Bragg, so I requested an assignment with the

82nd Aviation Regiment and was fortunate enough to be picked up. Not that we get to see each other all that often, but it makes my mother feel better knowing we're within shouting distance of each other."

"Well, it makes sense in hindsight," she said, and a ghost of a smile tilted her lips. "I actually tried to hit on you yesterday, after we arrived, but in fact I was hitting on your brother."

"Yeah," he said darkly. "I heard. When you called me Chase, all I could think was that you might have slept with him, thinking he was me. You were clearly upset, and I knew he was on the base, so I jumped to conclusions."

"You really freaked me out," she said, straightening up. "When you asked me what your name was and wanted to know when we had met, I was convinced you'd suffered some sort of brain damage."

Chance laughed softly. "I can see why you thought that. I must have seemed a little unbalanced." Reaching over, he laced his fingers with hers, gratified when she didn't pull away. "I'm sorry. I should have come clean with you that night at the airfield about being a pilot."

She made a self-deprecating sound and rolled her eyes. "Me and my big mouth. I said some pretty horrible things about pilots, and I don't blame you for keeping quiet. After my anti-aviator rant, you were probably too terrified to tell me the truth."

"I was *not* terrified," he said firmly. "I didn't tell you that I was a pilot because I didn't want you to beat yourself up over what we'd done, not when it was so freaking great." He was quiet for a moment, debating. He squeezed her fingers gently. "But what I really didn't want was for you to hate me. Or yourself."

She turned to look at him, and her expression softened. "You told me that you hoped I wouldn't think badly of you if we ever met again."

"Look, if you would just give me a chance—"

A hard gust of wind hit the side of the helicopter, peppering the exterior with sand and small rocks and startling them both. Through the windshield, the world was an impenetrable haze of brownish-yellow fog.

"Christ, this thing could go on for days," Chance muttered. "I hate being grounded."

Jenna released his hand and stood up, keeping her head low, but he was unprepared when she straddled his thighs and looped her hands around his neck. Under the fine coating of dust that covered her skin and workout clothes, he could smell her fragrance.

"When I saw your brother yesterday at Kalagush," she said quietly, looking directly into his eyes, "and I thought he was you...my first reaction was absolute shock."

He gave a huff of laughter. "I can understand why."

"When you acted as if you didn't recognize me, I thought you were sending me a clear message that you weren't interested," she said wryly. "That, or you were trying to keep our previous relationship a secret from your men."

Reaching up, he tucked a loose strand of hair behind her ear. "That's what *you* would do, not me."

He deliberately didn't make any comment about being interested or not. He'd already told her how he felt about that night, and he'd all but said he'd like a repeat performance. The next move was up to her, although he wasn't sure how he would react if she insisted they couldn't see each other again. He hoped he would accept her decision with grace, but just the thought caused an uncomfortable tightening in his chest.

She gave him a rueful smile. "Well, I'd already decided I wanted to see you again."

Chance pulled back a bit and studied her face. "That was when you thought I was special ops. Would you have felt the same way if you'd known I was an Apache pilot?"

Jenna averted her gaze and silence stretched between them until Chance was sure she wasn't going to answer. She dropped her arms from around his neck and plucked moodily at the front of his T-shirt. "I'd like to think so, but the truth is…I'm not sure."

"Well, at least you're honest," he said drily.

"Even believing you were special ops, I had to think long and hard about whether I really wanted to hook up with you again."

Chance gave her a lopsided grin, even as something fisted low in his gut. "That bad, huh?"

When she raised her gaze to his, she wasn't smiling. "No…that *good*. But the last time I saw you, I got the distinct sense that you couldn't wait to get rid of me."

"Not true," he retorted gently. "I had just had this amazing night with you, only to discover I was the embodiment of everything you were determined to avoid. If it makes you feel any better, I didn't get any sleep that night."

"Good," she murmured, "because neither did I."

Jenna's gaze dropped briefly to his mouth, and he heard her breathing hitch. Chance's body tightened under her sensual scrutiny and it took all his effort not to lean forward and kiss her.

"I really wanted to see you again, but I knew I needed to tell you the truth about what I do for the army," he admitted. "It took me a couple of days, then I went over to your battalion to look for you, only to find out you had deployed."

He knew he'd surprised her. "You came looking for me?"

"I did, yeah. I missed you by just a few hours." He studied her face. "So imagine my surprise when, two months later, I find out that not only are you here at Kabul, but you actually propositioned my damned brother!"

Jenna cringed. "Sorry. I thought he was you—special ops."

"Understood. And now you know that I'm not." He dipped his head to look directly into her eyes. "So...?"

"So now I understand why you asked me not to think badly of you if we ever met again." She paused. "Well, I don't."

Relief swamped Chance so strongly that he had to fight to keep the silly grin off his face. She hadn't actually said that she'd revised her opinion of male pilots in general, but the fact that she wasn't throwing him out of her helicopter was more than he'd hoped for. Now he arched one eyebrow. "Really. Maybe you could, uh, demonstrate how you do feel."

Jenna settled herself more fully on his lap and glanced at his watch. "It's oh-six-hundred hours. Don't you have to report for duty?"

Chance wanted to groan at the sensation of her smooth thighs straddling his bare legs, and the sexy expression in her eyes. "Not until oh-eight-hundred hours," he finally managed. "That gives us two hours—

give or take a few minutes—in which you can show me exactly how much you don't think badly of me."

"Then we'd better hurry," she murmured. "This could take awhile."

7

IN FOR AN INCH, IN FOR a mile, Jenna decided, or at least a solid eight inches, if her memory was correct. She'd already had sex with Chase—er, Chance. Granted, she hadn't known he was a pilot at the time, but it seemed hypocritical to let that stop her now. She still had a hard time believing he was actually a pilot, and she cringed when she recalled the derogatory things she'd said. No wonder he hadn't told her what he did for a living; she would have kept her mouth shut, too.

She'd been shocked when he'd introduced her to his twin brother, but there had also been a part of her that was secretly relieved, since it meant he hadn't really rejected her when she'd propositioned him in the hangar. She supposed she should be grateful that Chase hadn't taken her up on her offer.

Recalling how she had spent most of her life trying to win the approval of her father, she still had no intention of allowing her relationship with Chance to become more than casual. But she didn't see any reason why she shouldn't enjoy whatever he might be willing to share with her. Once the sandstorm was over, she would return to Kandahar, and their paths would separate once again. Kabul Air Base was one of her routine stops when transporting troops, and she'd spent the night here on several occasions. The opportunity to see Chance again was excellent, and provided they were discreet, there was no reason why they couldn't continue what they had started in that field at Fort Bragg.

Her legs were long enough that her feet easily reached the floor as she straddled his thighs, and she was close enough that her breasts almost brushed his chest. The sandstorm raged outside and the lighting in the helicopter was dim, but she could still make out the heated expression in his eyes. His hands rested at her waist, and his nearness created a chaos of sensations inside her. The way he looked at her made her feel both shy and confident, like she was the sexiest woman he'd ever seen and he couldn't wait to devour her. Now she realized it was that precise quality that had been missing when she'd crossed paths with his brother the day before. There had been none of the sexual awareness, none of the mutual attraction. In hindsight, she couldn't understand how she'd gotten them mixed up.

From her position on his lap, she couldn't fail to notice the growing evidence of his arousal beneath the soft fabric of his workout shorts, or the way his pupils had dilated so that his irises were nearly swallowed up by the blackness. Even his breathing had changed, and Jenna found her own ability to breathe compromised by his nearness.

"Jenna," he muttered, his gaze dropping to her mouth. Almost as if he couldn't help himself, he reached up and pulled her ponytail free, threading his fingers through her hair until it hung in loose waves around her face. He framed her jaw in his big hands and dipped his head, his lips just brushing her own.

As a kiss, it was no more than a tentative question, but when he drew slightly back, Jenna followed, seeking more of the elusive contact. Her hands came up to curl lightly around his wrists and urge him back.

"Please," she murmured on a soft exhale.

With a groan of defeat, Chance buried his hands in her hair and brought his mouth down on hers. This time, there was nothing tentative or hesitant about the way he kissed her. He consumed her, slanting his mouth hard across her own until she welcomed the hot, hungry thrust of his tongue. He licked at her, dragging an urgent response from her. The kiss was so carnal and sexy that heat exploded beneath her skin and raced along her nerve endings until every part of her body was on fire. She was only vaguely aware of scooting forward on his thighs and winding her arms around his neck, her fingers rubbing over the hard muscles of his shoulders and back.

"God, you feel good," she said against his mouth.

In answer, he bent her back over one arm and pushed her T-shirt upward, smoothing his hand across her bare skin until he encountered the edge of her bra. But that was no deterrent and, with one easy flick of his fingers, he released the front clasp, exposing her breasts. He broke their kiss long enough to pull back and admire her. His eyes glittered hotly as he bent his head and flicked one distended nipple with the tip of his tongue, causing a sharp stab of lust to knife through Jenna.

"Oh, yes," she breathed, spearing her fingers through his short hair and urging him to continue.

Chance complied, laving her breast with his tongue until finally, when Jenna thought she couldn't stand any more of the sensual torture, he drew the pebbled tip into his mouth, sucking hard and causing a rush of warm moisture between her thighs. She squirmed on his lap and he pushed a hand between her legs to cup her intimately through the material of her shorts.

"You're so damned soft," he muttered against her breast. "I want to see you."

Before she realized his intent, he stood up, lifting her with him and then turning until she reclined on the nylon seat, while he leaned over her. She made no protest when he dragged her T-shirt over her head, and then eased her bra off until she wore nothing but her shorts and her workout shoes. For a moment, he just stood and stared at her, and Jenna had to resist the urge to clap her hands over her breasts.

"Don't be embarrassed," he said gruffly, reading her thoughts. "You're gorgeous."

"What if somebody comes?" Her gaze slid to the window, where the outside visibility was absolutely zero.

"Nobody's coming out here to check on the choppers," he assured her. "Not in this weather. But just in case…"

Jenna watched as he made his way to each sliding door and secured a metal latch, locking the doors from the inside. Returning, he crouched in front of her with his hands on her bare thighs, and Jenna leaned forward to press a moist kiss against his mouth. He deepened the kiss, stroking her with his tongue and causing the tiny flames that licked along her skin to reignite. When he cupped her breasts, she almost groaned with pleasure at the sensation. He massaged her sensitized flesh and rolled her nipples between his fingers before squeezing them gently. His kiss, combined with his caresses, had her arching toward him, and she ran her palms over his shoulders and arms, before grasping the hem of his T-shirt and tugging it upward.

"My turn," she breathed against his lips, gratified when he reached behind his head and grasped a fistful of the shirt, dragging it off. Jenna knew her eyes went a little hazy, but honestly, the sight of his lean, supremely muscled torso took her breath away. She couldn't prevent her hands from drifting over his chest to explore the ridges of his abdomen, before sliding her arms around him and pressing her bare breasts against his warm skin.

She planted damp kisses along his neck before letting her lips follow the angle of his jaw until she encountered his ear. Taking his lobe between her teeth, she bit down gently and then soothed the area with her tongue until he turned his face, seeking her lips with his own. The kiss was hot and potent and so deep that their teeth scraped briefly. She heard a soft moaning sound and was shocked when she realized it came from her.

"Darlin'," he rasped, pulling slightly away to search her face, "I need to touch you."

Jenna sank back in the troop seat, her breasts heaving. There was no embarrassment now, only an urgent need that demanded fulfillment. Chance knelt on the hard floor between her knees, his hands at the waistband of her shorts. His face was taut, his attention riveted on her. In answer to his silent question, Jenna raised her hips and allowed him to tug both her shorts and her panties down over her hips and thighs. He pulled her sneakers off, too, until she sprawled completely naked on the small seat.

"Oh, man, you are so gorgeous," he breathed, his eyes searing her as he took in every inch of her exposed body. Jenna could feel the heat rising on her skin like a sunburn wherever his gaze touched her.

"You act like you've never seen me before." Her voice sounded breathless.

"I've never seen you like this before," he countered. "Besides, it was pretty damned dark that night by the flight line. But this—" he glanced at the windows "—this is like high noon by comparison. I feel like I'm seeing you for the first time."

Despite the haziness of the sandstorm, weak morning light filtered through the windows of the Black Hawk, outlining Chance's features and casting intriguing shadows across his toned body. Jenna felt as if she was seeing him for the first time, too, and only part of that was the result of discovering his true identity.

Now he eased her knees apart and slid a hand between her thighs to cup her. Jenna's sex throbbed with need, and she knew if he explored farther, he would find her slick with moisture. She was so aroused that part of her feared she would orgasm immediately.

With exquisite care, Chance slid a finger along her cleft. Jenna shivered with sensation and forced herself to remain still. But when he swirled his thumb through her wetness and then found the small rise of her clitoris, she nearly came out of the chair.

"Easy," he murmured. "How's this?"

The things that he was doing with his fingers defied description, and Jenna could only gasp in pleasure and let her head fall helplessly back against the seat. He was relentless, bringing her close to the brink of orgasm several times, but each time pulling back and denying her relief. The fact that she was completely nude and open to him while he was still partially clothed only heightened her excitement and lent a dark thrill of the forbidden to what they were doing.

"I want to eat you," he muttered, his attention fixed on the swollen flesh he stroked with his fingers.

His words caused her to clench her sex hard, and then he was dragging her hips to the very edge of the chair and pushing her thighs wide. He bent his head and kissed the inside of one knee, before skating up her leg. His fingers massaged her mons, arousing her but denying her any direct contact. When he reached the juncture of her thighs, he breathed deeply and then glanced up at her, his eyes dark with arousal.

"Christ, you smell good," he growled softly.

Before Jenna could prepare herself, he put his mouth on her, using his fingers to separate her slick folds and expose her to his greedy tongue. She groaned deeply, feeling herself swell even more at the sensation of his hot mouth on her sensitized flesh. But when he eased a finger into her and began to flick her clitoris with his tongue, she writhed helplessly in pleasure, feeling the irresistible build of an orgasm.

"Come for me," he rasped, and slid a second finger inside her.

His sexy demand, combined with the erotic things he was doing, was too much for Jenna, and with a strangled cry, she fragmented around him, her body shuddering with the intensity of her release. Even then, he didn't stop, laving her softly with his tongue until he'd drawn every last shiver from her spent body.

She pushed weakly at his head. "Stop, please," she gasped. "You're killing me."

He made a sound of regret and pulled away, wiping his hand across his mouth as he smiled at her with masculine pride. "That was unbelievable. I could do that all day."

Satiated as she was, his words caused a tight coiling in her abdomen and the inner muscles of her channel tightened.

"I want you inside me," she whispered.

His eyes grew languorous. "Oh, darlin'," he groaned. "Trust me, I want the same thing, but I didn't exactly come prepared." He rocked back on his heels and pulled his pockets inside out, showing her that they were empty. Beneath the soft fabric of his shorts, Jenna could see the evidence of his own arousal, and her mouth grew dry at the thought of releasing his stiff flesh.

"I'm on the Pill," she ventured. "So if that's what's worrying you…"

His expression grew taut. "I just had my military physical," he replied, his voice roughened with need, "and I can promise you that I'm completely clean."

"Then come inside me," she invited, and leaned back in the chair, allowing her legs to fall open. She watched, entranced, as Chance's breathing hitched and every muscle in his body seemed to tighten. He glanced around the stark interior of the Black Hawk, and Jenna could see that he was trying to figure out a way to make this work. Every surrounding surface was unforgiving metal, except for the troop seats.

"Come here," she said, shifting forward to the edge of the seat. Reaching out, she caught his hips and drew him toward her. She knew the precise moment when he understood her intent, and she watched in fascination as a dark flush of arousal stained his neck.

"You don't have to do this," he growled softly, watching her with eyes that glittered.

"Oh, I know." She smiled. "But I want to."

Slowly, she pulled him closer until he stood bracketed between her bare knees. Hooking her thumbs into the elastic waistband of his shorts, she drew them slowly downward, her breath catching as his erection sprang into view. He was full and heavy, as thick around as her wrist, and her mouth watered at the sight of him.

Jenna curled one hand around the base of his cock, feeling how he jumped against her palm, and smoothed the tip of one finger across the blunted head, where a bead of moisture beckoned her. He was hot and hard, and she could feel the blood churning beneath her fingers, causing him to swell even more.

"Oh, wow," she murmured, stroking the velvety skin. "You are really something." Glancing up at his face, she saw his expression was rigid, evidence of how tightly he controlled himself. "I wonder how you taste?"

Leaning forward, she ran her tongue over him, reveling in his sweet-salty taste. She heard him suck in a sharp breath, and then she slid her mouth over him, licking the length of him and drawing on him as if he was her favorite flavored Popsicle. Chance gave a deep grunt of pleasure and, reaching down, scooped her hair to one side so that he could watch. Peeking up the length of his body, Jenna saw he was holding on to an overhead grip with his free hand, as if he didn't quite trust his knees to support him. The expression on his face as he watched her was so incredibly sexy that she felt a rush of liquid heat pool at her center. Stroking him in concert with the movement of her lips, she used her free hand to cup and fondle his balls, feeling an intense satisfaction as they tightened in her palm.

"Oh, man," he groaned, "I'm not going to last much longer."

Jenna would have been happy for him to lose control right then, but he clearly had other ideas. Pulling free, he bent down and kissed her, before tugging her to her feet and taking her place on the troop seat.

"Here," he said, guiding her onto his lap, "let's try this."

Jenna straddled his hard thighs, bracing her hands on his shoulders as she levered herself over his straining cock. He helped her, lifting her up and using a hand to position himself at the entrance to her body. Slowly, Jenna lowered herself down, sighing in pleasure as he eased into her, inch by exquisite inch, until he completely stretched and filled her. When she was sitting flush against his thighs, his hard length buried inside her, she raised her gaze to his. What she saw in his eyes nearly took her breath away. His face was so rapt, so intent, that for a moment she could only stare helplessly back at him.

"Kiss me," she demanded softly.

He did, sliding his hands over her bare back and beneath the heavy fall of her hair to cradle her scalp as he fastened his mouth to hers. Their lips fused together in a moist, hungry mating that made her toes curl. He smelled like soap and clean sweat, and he tasted faintly of coffee and mint.

She wanted to eat him.

When he moved his hands to her rear and cupped her buttocks, she helped him by slowly moving up and down, feeling the hot, thick slide of his penis inside her. The inner muscles of her sex tightened around him, and when he squeezed her cheeks, she could feel the beginning of another orgasm.

"Oh, man," he groaned into her mouth, "you feel too good."

In answer, Jenna raised herself up until he was almost free of her body, and wound her arms around Chance's head, threading her fingers through his velvet-rough hair as she kissed him deeply. Then she lowered herself back onto his shaft. Her breasts were flattened against his chest, and as his fingers squeezed and massaged her bottom, she quickened the rhythm of her hips, meeting his upward thrusts with increasing urgency. The combination of his tongue in her mouth and his rigid length filling her was almost more than she could bear. But when he made a deep groaning noise of pleasure and tightened his grip on her cheeks, she knew he was close to climaxing.

Breaking the kiss, Jenna pulled slightly back to watch his face, entranced by his stark expression of pleasure-pain. His breathing came in harsh gasps, and when he looked into her eyes, Jenna felt something shift in her chest at the knowledge that she had done this to him.

"I'm coming," he managed to say through gritted teeth, and surged upward. At the same time, he slid a hand between their straining bodies to press a finger against her clitoris. Jenna actually felt him pulse strongly inside her, and she heard herself cry out in pleasure as her body fisted helplessly around his hard length. He kept his fingers on her until she stopped shuddering, and then she collapsed, boneless, against his chest. He held her tightly, one hand smoothing her hair as he murmured words of endearment.

Beneath her ear, she could hear the heavy, swift beat of his heart. He was still hard inside her, and she experienced a moment of panic when she wished—just for a second—that they could remain like this forever. She didn't want to return to reality, where romance was nothing more than an illusion—a few stolen moments inside a military helicopter. She wanted to pretend, at least for a little bit, that this meant something to both of them.

"Hey," Chance murmured against her hair. "You okay?"

She nodded, wanting to curl closer, but he was already disengaging himself from her arms. Reluctantly, Jenna stood, allowing him to withdraw from her. He searched the floor until he found her discarded handkerchief and gave it a couple of hard shakes before he silently handed it to her. Turning away from him, she quickly cleaned herself up while he found his shorts and began pulling them on.

Jenna didn't know what to say to him. The sex had been incredible, as she'd known it would be. But the man who had brought her such pleasure with so little effort was gone, and she hardly recognized the hard-eyed soldier who stood watching her moodily. She could almost guess what was coming, and she dressed swiftly, as if her clothing could offer her some kind of protection.

"We need to talk," he said bluntly, and Jenna knew there wasn't anything that could protect her from the truth.

8

CHANCE SCRUBBED A HAND over his face and lowered himself into one of the troop seats. Jenna watched him warily, and her gaze flicked once to the locked sliding doors. Given the right provocation, he realized she'd bolt again. He chose his words carefully.

"Look, I want you to know that I didn't plan for that to happen."

She nodded. "I do."

"But I'm not going to say I'm sorry, because it wouldn't be true."

Jenna looked away, silent. He knew she wasn't sorry, either. Hell, she'd all but initiated the encounter, but he was beginning to know enough about her to realize that she wouldn't welcome a reminder. Despite the fact the sex had been great, she probably considered it a huge mistake. He couldn't help wondering if she'd have felt differently had it been his brother who had come after her, and not him.

"I know you have this thing against pilots," he began, and put up a hand to forestall her when she would have protested. "I get it, I really do. But we're in completely separate units, and I think that if you'd just give it a chance, we could make this work."

Her gaze snapped back to his, and he could see the dismay in their hazel depths. "Make what work? A booty call every time I pass through Kabul?"

Chance kept his voice patient. "This doesn't have to be about sex, Jenna. Could we at least try to get to know each other before you completely scrap any chance at a relationship?"

She hesitated, her inner conflict written on her face so clearly that he almost took pity on her. Almost.

"You think you know all there is to know about me because I'm a pilot, and therefore I must be like all the other pilots you've met," Chance replied tightly, struggling to control his patience. "But the truth is, you don't know me at all." Stepping toward her, he cupped her cheek in one hand, gratified when she didn't pull away. "I know what it's like to have something to prove, darlin'."

She half turned her face into his hand. "I don't know what you're talking about."

"I think you do," he said. He could almost feel her softening. "Why didn't you tell me your father is Erik Larson?"

"That has nothing to do with anything."

Chance wasn't convinced. "Doesn't it? Your dad happens to be one of the most heroic helicopter pilots of all time, and you end up following in his footsteps. It's natural that people are going to compare you, and that you're going to feel you need to live up to his expectations. Or his reputation."

She gave a soft laugh. "And what would you know about it? Look at you. You're practically perfect."

"Plenty," he assured her. "Did you happen to notice

my bigger-than-life brother? He's always been the best at whatever he puts his mind to, and I'm not going to lie and tell you it's easy to be his twin. People have always compared us, and no matter how much I tried to be like him, I always came up short. Even now, you should see how people react when they hear he's a special ops commando, while I'm a helicopter pilot. It's like I'm fifteen years old all over again."

Chance recalled those competitive years in high school, when he'd struggled to best his brother in everything. But Chase had been a superlative athlete and student, and it had seemed, no matter how well Chance did, he inevitably ended up in his brother's shadow. So he'd chosen a different path. He'd become an adrenaline junkie, and where Chase had garnered attention for the way he tackled and overcame every challenge with deliberate precision, Chance had become notorious as a risk taker. He'd liked fast cars and easy girls, and if his family had disapproved of his choices, at least they were taking notice of him.

But the need to compete with Chase had become so ingrained in him that when his brother had announced his plans to join the military, Chance was right there beside him. It had been the best choice he'd ever made, and had enabled him to finally step out of his brother's shadow and excel at something in his own right.

Was the need to compete with Chase still there? Oh, yeah. But now the rivalry was friendly, and Chance no longer worried about living up to his family's expectations. He was living up to his own, and that's what mattered.

Jenna looked at him, speculation gleaming in her eyes. "I would have thought just the opposite was true—that your brother would have come up short when compared to you."

Chance grinned. "I'll take that as a compliment. But I guess what I'm trying to say is that you don't have to be perfect. Your father was an exception, and it would be unrealistic to expect to be just like him."

Jenna gave a derisive snort. "Trust me, I do not aspire to be like my father."

There was an underlying issue there, but Chance knew better than to pursue it. He recalled something she'd said during their first night together; that her negative opinion of pilots was based on a lifetime of observation. Had she been referring to her father? He knew plenty of guys in the military who were exceptional soldiers but lousy husbands and fathers. Had Erik Larson fallen into that category? If so, it explained a lot about her attitude.

"Okay," he conceded. "Where do we go from here? Because I'm not going to lie to you. I want to see you again. I'm not talking booty calls, either. I know you come through Kabul every couple of weeks and there's always the chance that I could fly to Kandahar once in a while." He shrugged. "We could just grab a bite to eat, or maybe catch a movie at the rec center."

Jenna studied him for a moment before turning away to stare moodily out the window. Chance wished he knew what was going on in her head. He didn't miss how she drummed her fingers against her thigh, and he knew she was considering his offer. He realized that he'd told her the truth when he'd said he wanted to get to know her. The sex was amazing, but he wanted more. He wanted to know what made her tick; he wanted to know what she liked. He wanted to know why she'd become a pilot, and why she avoided guys in the military. Most of all, he wanted to know if they could make a go of a real relationship. From what he'd seen so far, he believed they could.

She turned around to face him, and in the instant before she guarded her expression, he saw the vulnerability in her eyes. "Okay, fine."

"What?" He was certain he'd misheard.

"I agree," she said smoothly. "Since we're speaking candidly, then I admit that I want to see you again, too. I'd be crazy not to."

Chance felt something shift in his chest. He had looked for an argument at the very least. The last thing he'd expected was for her to agree so quickly. He couldn't stop the grin that spread over his face.

"That's great."

"I do have one condition."

He only just prevented his shoulders from sagging with defeat. He'd known it couldn't be so easy. "Okay, I'm listening."

"If I agree to see you again, it's on the condition that this remains casual."

"Define *casual*."

"As in, no commitments and we're both free to see other people."

Chance bit back the snarl of denial that sprang to his lips. Just the thought of Jenna with anyone else unleashed something feral inside him. But he knew if he protested and insisted on any kind of exclusive relationship, she'd balk and he'd never see her again.

"So in other words," he said, allowing a trace of sarcasm to color his voice, "we're back to the booty calls."

"Call it whatever you like, but those are my conditions."

"Why?" he demanded. "Why are you so determined to keep this superficial?"

He watched as a range of emotions crossed her face, almost too fleeting to identify. Hurt. Indecision. Determination. Despite what she'd said about never having dated a pilot, Chance was convinced that someone had treated her bad.

"Look," she said tightly. "It's not personal. I just prefer to keep it casual, and not have everything else get in the way."

"Everything else? What—our careers? Our families? Our feelings?"

Jenna sighed and pushed her fingers through her hair, sweeping it back from her face. "I just think it would be easier if we kept everything else out of it. I don't want to compete with you."

What the...?

Chance stared at her in bemusement, but there was a part of him that understood her fear. Not that he believed for one second that he would ever want to compete with her, but he'd seen it happen with other pilots. The fact that she believed he would fall into that category irritated the hell out of him.

"Thanks for the vote of confidence," he said drily. "Look, I'm not saying that it doesn't happen, but it wouldn't happen with us."

Jenna gave him a doubtful look. "Oh, no? What makes you so sure?"

He grinned. "Because my job is definitely more dangerous and more important than yours. And even though I've never seen you fly, I know I'm the better pilot." As her mouth fell open, he laughed. "Relax. I'm totally kidding. I don't believe any of that for a second."

Even saying the words aloud sounded arrogant and

he hoped that by teasing her a little, she'd realize how ridiculous it was for her to think he'd act that way.

She shrugged and gave him a sheepish smile. "Well, if it's any consolation, I don't, either. But I do believe we're better off avoiding a committed relationship."

"How do you figure?"

She didn't meet his eyes. "Speaking from my own experience, pilots have this weird inability to remain monogamous. Even though you think you want a relationship, eventually you'd have the urge to explore other waters. I just think that if we both acknowledge that now, we'll save ourselves a little bit of heartache down the road."

"You really do believe that?" he asked, incredulous. Admittedly, he hadn't done much in his six years as a pilot to dispel the reputation of being a player, but this was different. *He* was different. He was finally at a place in his life where he was happy with who he was, and he no longer felt he had anything to prove.

"I haven't seen any evidence to the contrary," she replied stiffly.

Give me a chance.

He almost said the words aloud, and just barely bit them back. No way was he going to beg. He wanted to show her how wrong her perceptions were, but he could see by the expression on her face that if he continued to argue with her, she would walk away. He told himself to take whatever she was willing to give, and show her that he was different. Eventually, she'd learn to trust him.

"What about you?" he asked. "You're a pilot. Do you fall into that same category? Are you unable to maintain a monogamous relationship?"

She gave him a faint smile. "I've never wanted to, so it's never been an issue."

Chance didn't like the implications of her words. He didn't want to think about her with anyone else, doing the things she'd done with him. He was an idiot. Every brain cell that still functioned told him to walk away from this, because to do anything else was just asking for trouble. But then again, he'd never been one to take the easy way out. He'd always been a risk taker, and this was no exception. He could make this work.

"Okay, fine," he said, spreading his arms wide. "I agree to your terms. We keep it casual. No strings, no commitments."

"Really?" She narrowed her eyes at him, clearly suspicious.

"I'm getting a distinct feeling of déjà vu here," he said, smiling. "I'm pretty sure we had this conversation that night at Pope airfield."

"Yes, but I didn't know you were a pilot, and we both thought that was just a one-time hookup. I never expected to see you again."

"Which begs another question. Is this a public relationship, or do we keep it under wraps?" He knew from her shuttered expression what her answer would be. "Under wraps. Got it. So we can forget about grabbing a movie or a bite to eat, huh? This is strictly about sex. I think your roommate might have already guessed there's something going on."

"I trust Laura," Jenna said, "but I really prefer that no one else in my unit—or yours—knows about us."

"Shouldn't be a problem," he said, hating the conditions she imposed but he was smart enough to keep his mouth shut. "I have my own housing unit, so as long as we're discreet..." He glanced at his watch. "I'd suggest we head over to the chow hall and grab some breakfast, but that's probably out of the question, right?"

Jenna pressed her lips together. "Not a good idea. I mean, technically there would be no reason for us to even know each other, and I'd rather not give people something to talk about."

Chance thought about her precipitous flight from the gym and how he had chased her into the dust storm. He wasn't stupid enough to remind her that they'd probably stirred up all kinds of gossip, not to mention the fact that the two mechanics in the hangar knew he'd come out here looking for her and hadn't returned for nearly an hour. Would that generate talk? You bet. But he just nodded.

"I'll take off, then. You might want to wait a few minutes before you head out." He hesitated, not wanting to leave her, although he knew there were other, more practical reasons why they shouldn't be seen leaving the MH-60 together. They could both find themselves in a lot of trouble if anyone discovered what they had been doing. "You'll be okay? The visibility is zero out there. It would be easy to get disoriented, lose your way."

She drew in a deep breath and smiled, but it was clearly forced. No matter what she might say, he'd bet money on the fact that she wasn't any happier about this arrangement than he was. She might think she wanted to keep it casual, but he had a feeling she wasn't a casual type of gal.

"You go," she said. "I'll be fine, really."

"Okay, then." He stepped toward her and caught her face in both hands, covering her mouth with his in a possessive kiss. He knew he'd surprised her, but he didn't pull away until he felt her body sag against his, and her hands crept to his shoulders. Only when she was returning his kiss did he step back, noting her bereft expression with satisfaction. "I'll see you around."

Before he could change his mind, he swiftly unlocked the door and slid it back, stepping out into the scalding wind and closing the door behind him. Leaving her like this went against his better judgment. But he'd play by her rules.

For now.

9

JENNA SAT ALONE IN THE helicopter after Chance left, trying to collect her thoughts and pull together the shreds of her shaky self-composure. No guy had ever made her respond the way he had, as if he knew her body better than she did. And what was it about him that made her want to peel her clothes off the second he drifted into her orbit? Sure, he was good-looking and had a body honed to perfection, but so did a lot of other guys, and she'd never found herself spread naked across their laps. And in a military helicopter, no less! She hated to think what might have happened if anyone had discovered them. She prided herself on her self-control, yet it seemed whenever Chance was near, she lost it completely.

Could she really have a casual relationship with him? She recalled the intensity of his kiss, the confidence and skill he'd shown in handling her body. There was absolutely nothing casual about the guy. He radiated a vibrant energy that was impossible to ignore. She still couldn't believe she'd had sex with him in a Black Hawk. If her commanding officer ever found out, she'd find herself grounded for a lot longer than just a few days.

Was this how her mother had felt when she'd first met Jenna's dad? Jenna had heard the story enough times. Lisa Colbert had just graduated from college and had rented a summer cottage on Cape Cod with her roommates. On a whim, they'd decided to book a one-hour helicopter tour of the Cape and islands, and Erik Larson had been their pilot. But when the tour was over, he'd asked Lisa for a date. At thirty-five, he'd been nearly thirteen years older than her. As handsome and confident as he'd been, he must have seemed bigger than life. He'd flown her to the island of Martha's Vineyard for dinner, and then back to Cape Cod, where they'd been nearly inseparable for the next two months. And when the summer had drawn to a close, he'd proposed.

But, according to her mom, Erik Larson was an adrenaline junkie, and when he wasn't flying, he looked for other ways to get his fix of excitement. She'd said there was an emptiness inside him that neither she nor Jenna could fill. He drank too much, and he liked to gamble. And after Jenna's mom had become pregnant, he'd begun to have affairs. Jenna recalled the bitter arguments and her mother's tears. Her father would leave the house and sometimes wouldn't return for days. Those were the times that scared Jenna the most. When she was older, she'd learned that during those periods, he'd take one of his helicopters and fly to New Jersey, usually to the casinos, where he'd indulge in a spree of drinking, gambling and womanizing.

Her parents had finally divorced when she was eight years old, and Jenna had spent every subsequent summer on Cape Cod with her dad. He'd tried to be a responsible father, but he hadn't been very good at relationships. What he was good at was flying helicopters, and he'd had Jenna behind the controls of a small Bell 47 before she was a teenager. At first, she hadn't loved flying. In fact, it had scared the hell out of her. But she'd desperately wanted to please her father so she'd stuck with it. When they were in the cockpit together, she'd had his undivided attention. It was the only time that Jenna felt he really saw her as anything other than a responsibility. He'd been a patient instructor, and when she'd finally mastered the controls, she'd actually believed that he was proud of her. And what had begun as a chore had eventually transformed into a true love for flying.

Erik Larson still operated a small charter helicopter company, providing aerial tours of Cape Cod and the islands, survey flights, photography services and occasional lift work. Since her mother had remarried, Jenna actually spent more of her free time on Cape Cod, helping run the charter business, than she did with her mother and stepfather. But she felt no closer to her father now than she had when she was a child. In fact, the only time she really felt a connection to him was when they were flying, or talking about flying.

Chance wasn't at all like her father. She knew that. Her dad had lived with a lot of internal demons that had made it difficult, if not impossible, for him to have normal relationships. But Chance had a lot in common with the pilots she'd known since she'd joined the military. Men who put their careers ahead of their families. She didn't really blame them, because the military demanded complete and total commitment. Which was why she couldn't see herself married to a pilot.

Eventually, she wanted to have a family, but only

when she was ready to put her own military career behind her, and only when she met the right guy— preferably a civilian. So it was important that she not develop any attachment to Chance. She knew instinctively that the military was his life. He'd never voluntarily leave. Which was why their relationship could only ever be casual.

When she felt like she'd regained some perspective, she made her way carefully back to her housing unit, skirting the hangar and glad for the extra pair of goggles she'd found in the cockpit. The dust storm showed no signs of abating. If anything, it had grown worse, and the wind-propelled sand stung as it struck her exposed skin. By the time she reached her hut, she was coated in dust and nearly gagging from the amount of sand she had ingested.

"There you are!" Laura exclaimed as Jenna burst through the door and closed it hard against the wind. "We're supposed to be over at the operations shack in fifteen minutes."

Despite the fact all aircraft were grounded, crew members were required to sit through an in-brief each morning. But surely she hadn't been gone that long? Jenna glanced at her watch, shocked to see how much time had passed since she'd left to go to the gym. She wouldn't even have time to shower. Laura was already fully dressed and impatient to leave.

"Okay," Jenna assured her. "I'll be ready in ten. Why don't you head on over and I'll be right behind you."

Laura arched an eyebrow. "I guess I don't have to ask if your boyfriend found you. You have razor burn on your face."

Before Jenna could protest that Chance was not her boyfriend, Laura pulled her goggles and scarf on and stepped out into the storm. With a muttered curse, Jenna quickly stripped, grateful to have the small hut to herself. She used a water bottle to wash up, examining her face in the small mirror next to her bed. Laura was right; the area around her mouth and jaw looked slightly abraded. Even her lips looked bruised, and Jenna's body tingled at the memory of Chance's kisses.

Shaking the dust out of her hair, she pulled it back into a neat braid and pinned it into place, before swiftly yanking on her uniform and boots. With five minutes left to spare, she pulled on her goggles and left the B-Hut at a dead run, bending her head into the dry wind and using a clean handkerchief to protect her nose and mouth.

She was the last one to arrive at the operations shack, a small wooden structure near the flight line, where pilots assembled each morning for mission assignments.

There were already a dozen or more crew members standing around the briefing table. She recognized several of them from her previous visits to Kabul Airbase, but only knew a couple of them personally. With the exception of Laura, they were all square-jawed men, including Captain Kevin "Mongo" McLaughlin, the only other Black Hawk pilot from her unit. He nodded at her as she entered the room, and she didn't miss the appreciative glances she drew from several of the other men as she threaded her way through the assembled group.

She was acutely aware that Chance leaned against the far wall, arms crossed over his chest. She refused to look directly at him, and chose a spot along the same wall, where she would be out of his direct line of vision. She didn't know if she could keep her emotions from showing on her face, and the last thing she needed was to fuel speculation that there was something going on between them.

"Hey, honey, you lost?" one of the younger pilots called to her with a cheeky grin.

"Nope, I'm exactly where I should be," she replied easily, "but I believe the preschool is located on the other side of the base." She smiled sweetly. "Just in case *you're* lost."

There was a collective hooting of laughter and ribald jokes as the junior pilot accepted the jibe in good humor.

"You do know this is the pilots' briefing room, right?" asked the man standing directly beside her, a smirk tilting his mouth as he assessed her.

Jenna could have turned so that he could see the aviator insignia on her shoulder, but before she could respond, Laura spoke up from his other side. "Captain Larson landed her MH-60 in complete brownout conditions, in a space no bigger than this conference table," she informed the room. "She was flying helos before most of you were out of grade school."

"You're a pilot?" the square-jawed man next to her asked, eyebrows raised.

"I am."

"Yeah, but can she hover?" The young pilot was openly leering now.

Learning how to hover was notoriously difficult, and one of the last maneuvers that a new pilot mastered. But there was no mistaking the sexual innuendo in the man's tone.

"Yeah, long enough to fire a Stinger missile at your dumb ass," Captain McLaughlin retorted, giving Jenna a friendly wink.

There was laughter, but several of the men stepped forward to introduce themselves and shake her hand.

"Okay, folks, listen up. I'm Lieutenant Colonel Daley, your tactical operations officer." A burly man with a bald head and piercing blue eyes entered the room and dropped a flight ops notebook onto the surface of the table with a loud thud. The room grew silent. "We have some visiting crew members with us today, so welcome. I'd advise the majority of you to make yourselves comfortable, since you won't be going anywhere anytime soon. This sandstorm is more than a mile high and a hundred miles wide, with sustained winds of sixty-plus miles per hour."

There were groans of disappointment as he went on to explain that the magnitude of the sandstorm meant that nearly all aircraft would continue to be grounded, at least through the next day. Jenna understood the damage that blowing sand could do to the helicopter engines, but there was a part of her that was as anxious as the other pilots to be in the air and away from here.

Away from temptation.

Away from Chance, with his easy grin and his made-for-sex physique. Jenna knew her ability to resist him was close to zero, and she suspected that if she spent too much time in his company, it would only get more difficult to keep their relationship casual. She found everything about him appealing, and that scared the hell out of her.

"You said 'most of us' would be grounded, sir," ventured the junior pilot. "Does that mean some of us won't? That you need a pilot?"

"I need a Black Hawk pilot with experience flying in brownout conditions." The tac ops officer looked up from the flight book and scanned the room.

Jenna's hand had shot into the air almost before he
had finished his sentence, and now she saw that Kevin
also had a finger raised in acknowledgment. The tac
ops officer gave Jenna a sharply assessing look, then
flicked his attention to the other pilot. "You have experience flying in brownout conditions, McLaughlin?"

"Affirmative, sir."

"Good. We have a high-value package that needs to
be delivered, ASAP. You'll transport the package and
then continue on to Kandahar." He glanced at his flight
book. "Rawlins and Fuller, you'll fly first and second
escort and then return to Kabul when the sandstorm
abates."

Jenna couldn't help herself. "Sir," she interjected, "I
can fly this mission. With all due respect, I have more
experience with brownout conditions than McLaughlin does." She didn't add that she had more experience,
period. She sensed Kevin's astonishment, but didn't
look over at him.

The tac ops officer nodded. "Understood, Larson,
but I've made my decision. McLaughlin has this assignment."

Jenna nodded, forcing herself to accept his decision with as much grace as she could muster. Leaning
slightly forward, she glanced along the wall to where
Chance stood. He'd already acknowledged the order
and was pulling his crew together, giving quiet direc-
tions for a maintenance check of the aircraft. The tac
ops officer dismissed the remaining crew members and
gathered Kevin and the Apache pilots together at the
briefing table.

Dismay and disappointment washed over Jenna as
she realized that Chance would depart Kabul Air Base
that very day, perhaps within hours. She might not see

him again before the storm let up and she returned to Kandahar.

Despite the fact she had just been thinking about the inherent danger in spending too much time in his company, there was a part of her that had been anticipating the coming night, wondering if Chance might ask her to spend it with him in his housing unit. Now that wouldn't be an option, and Jenna couldn't believe how let down she felt.

Looking at him, she could see his head was completely in the game. The mission came first, which was right. That's how it needed to be. She'd have responded exactly the same way if she had been given the assignment. There was no way she wanted to explore her own feelings of abandonment; it wasn't as if he had a choice about leaving. But she realized that when she was with Chance, she felt vitalized. Less than an hour earlier, she couldn't wait to leave both him and Kabul behind because she was afraid of becoming too attached to him. Now, knowing that he would be gone made her want to leave even more. Without Chance, it was just another military base.

"Hey. You okay?

Drawn out of her glum thoughts, Jenna turned to see Laura looking at her. "Yeah, I'm good," she replied, forcing a smile. "C'mon, let's get some breakfast."

As they left the briefing room, her gaze flashed one last time to Chance, but he was deep in discussion with the other pilots. He didn't notice when she followed Laura out of the briefing room and into the tiny lobby area. Through the small, dirty window, Jenna could see that the air outside was thick with dust and tinged an orange-red, so dense it would be difficult to see your own hand extended in front of your face. Chance would have a difficult time flying in these conditions. His flight instruments would keep him from crashing into a mountainside, but the real danger lay in the damage that the blowing sand could do to his engine. The pilots would need to fly above the storm to avoid that risk, but they would have no visibility to the ground.

Without having to ask, Jenna knew the high-value package was likely a detainee from the nearby prison. Whoever he was, he must be important for the army to risk sending three valuable aircraft into a sandstorm to deliver him. She'd transported her own share of enemy combatants in the weeks that she'd been in Afghanistan, but never during brownout conditions, although she had no doubt that she could fulfill the mission as well as McLaughlin. She didn't know what kind of experience he had, but she told herself she would not take it as a personal affront. The military needed a Black Hawk to transport their package, and Daley had chosen him as the pilot. End of story.

"Larson!"

Jenna turned to see Chance rounding the corner of the table and making a beeline toward her, his face set in determined lines. Without warning, her blood surged strongly through her veins and she strove for an expression of polite interest. There was no point in giving the other pilots any reason for gossip. Chance caught her by the upper arm and drew her aside.

"Hey," he said quietly, "are you okay?"

She made a sound of annoyance and pulled her arm free. "Why does everyone keep asking me that? Of course I am."

"Anyone could see you wanted this mission, but I'm just as happy to have you stay here."

Jenna shot him a disgruntled look. "I'm sure you are, but just to be clear, I *am* capable of flying this mission."

Chance gave a philosophical shrug. "I don't know why the colonel chose McLaughlin over you, but he must have his reasons."

Jenna remained unconvinced, but was too professional to say so. "Fine. Is there something you wanted to tell me?"

"Yes. This won't take me all day. I plan on being back here before nightfall."

Jenna raised her eyebrows. "What are you saying?"

His lips compressed in a clear expression of frustration and he glanced around quickly before lowering his voice. "I'll come to your hut when I get back. If this thing does clear up in the next day or so, you'll be given the all clear to head back to Kandahar. I don't want you to leave without seeing you again." When she didn't immediately respond, he tipped his head to look directly into her eyes. "I'll come see you as soon as I return. Is that okay?"

Jenna swallowed, and a frisson of anticipation fingered its way along her spine. If she had been selected for the mission instead of McLaughlin, she would be traveling on to Kandahar Air Base, and she might not have an opportunity to see Chance again for several weeks. The knowledge that she could get her night with him after all more than made up for not being chosen, and it released an explosion of butterflies in her stomach. She didn't trust herself to speak, so she just nodded.

"Good." He squeezed her arm gently. "Then I'll see you later."

He returned to the briefing room and Jenna might

have stood there watching him indefinitely had Laura not waved a hand in front of her nose. "Earth to Jenna."

Jenna snapped her attention back to her surroundings. "Sorry," she murmured. "C'mon, let's get some breakfast."

They crossed the compound to the dining facility, their goggles and scarves pulled tight over their faces. It wasn't until they were seated at a table in the corner with their food that Laura spoke again.

"So what was that all about?"

"What?" Jenna bit into a piece of toast and assumed what she hoped was an innocent expression.

Laura snorted, clearly unimpressed. "Oh, c'mon. You go to the gym, and less than an hour later, Mr. Hottie comes pounding on my door, looking a little desperate. Another hour goes by and then you show up with all the signs that you've just been royally worked over. In a good way, of course." She arched a dark eyebrow. "I'm not judging you. I actually think it's kinda cool. But what happened to your no-men-in-uniform motto?"

Jenna took a sip of strong, hot coffee. "As a matter of fact, he wasn't in uniform." She smiled. "Just the opposite. And that's all I'm saying."

Laura narrowed her eyes. "Okay, I get it. You don't want to share. That's fine, but I hope you know what you're doing. You've always been so adamant about avoiding pilots, and I don't want to see you get hurt."

Jenna gave her a brief smile. "No worries. We're both in agreement that this is just about sex. No commitments, no expectations of anything more. We're keeping it casual."

"Uh-huh." Laura sat back in her seat and considered Jenna before picking up her mug and taking a sip of her own coffee. "Let me know how that works for you, *chica*."

Jenna didn't answer, because there was a part of her that already suspected it wasn't going to work well.

10

THE TACTICAL OPERATIONS officer hadn't exaggerated about the magnitude of the sandstorm. After he and the other pilots had climbed above the storm, Chance could see how truly massive it was, extending below him as far as the eye could see. The Black Hawk that they escorted flew just beneath and to the right of his own aircraft, while the second Apache took up the rear. The package they were transporting was a high-ranking Afghan cleric, and he was under the watchful eye of no less than six military police and two men who Chance suspected were CIA.

They would deliver him to a forward operating base, or FOB, one hundred miles southwest of Kabul. Forward operating bases were typically considered to be the front line of combat action, and were in stark contrast to the heavily fortified and bustling main bases, like Kabul and Kandahar. They were often remote and the living conditions were harsh by any standards. This particular FOB was rumored to be a CIA stronghold, and Chance could well imagine what the *package* would endure once he was delivered into their hands.

They'd been flying for less than an hour when they

neared the base and began their descent. Unlike the Black Hawk helicopter, the Apache did not have a passenger compartment. There was only a tandem cockpit large enough to seat a two-man crew. Chase sat in the rear seat, slightly above his copilot/gunner, Warrant Officer Mike "Fishhead" Harrell. The Apache was designed purely as an attack aircraft, armed to the teeth with a 30 mm chain gun, missiles and rockets. Chase and his gunner sat on top of enough firepower to destroy a small city, and just the sight of an Apache helicopter was usually enough to deter any insurgents.

As they approached the FOB, Chance could see the dense sandstorm hadn't yet reached this region. They'd been flying with low visibility for the past thirty of forty miles, ahead of the storm front. While the air here was tinged with an orange hue from the storm, they could still see the surrounding landscape, although he suspected that would change as the day progressed and the front drew closer.

Now the FOB came into view several miles ahead of them, bordered by low hills and jutting rocks. Chance scanned the area, alert for any signs of trouble. Sangin was notorious for being one of the most dangerous spots in Afghanistan. In the Black Hawk, the door gunner sat with his rifle poised, ready to respond if a threat was detected. Although the tac ops officer had assured them that the transport of the high-value package had been kept under tight wraps, there was always a possibility that information had leaked out to the local tribal leaders. Numerous local nationals worked on the American bases in Afghanistan, and although the U.S. did background checks on each of them, history had proven that not all were trustworthy. Over his headphones, he heard the Black Hawk pilot, Captain "Mongo" McLaughlin, contact the FOB.

"Sangin Ground, Alpha-Three-One-Six-Zero-Foxtrot, four miles out, north by northeast, with two Apache escorts. ETA is five minutes. Over."

"Sangin Ground to Alpha-Three-One-Six-Zero-Foxtrot, ETA acknowledged. Use south ramp. Over."

Out of the corner of his eye, Chance saw a bright flash on the ground, coming somewhere from the rocky hills to their left. A white plume arced into the sky, headed directly toward them.

"Incoming SAM at nine o'clock—deploy countermeasures!" he barked into his headset.

Immediately, the air was filled with a brilliant burst of light as each aircraft launched its diversionary flares. Chance watched as the surface-to-air missile turned, moving fast, and expended itself on contact with one of the flares. The resulting explosion was close enough that the shock waves buffeted the helicopter.

"That was just a little too close," muttered Fishhead, peering through the windshield. "Where the hell did it come from?"

"Let's go in for a closer look," Chance suggested. Even as he said the words, a burst of gunfire exploded from the ground beneath them. "Taking fire, breaking right!"

"Where is it? Where is it?" This came from his wingman, Captain Tony "Teacup" Fuller, the pilot of the second Apache. They'd been roommates during flight school and had been stationed in the same unit together. They'd flown more missions together than Chance could keep track of, and there wasn't another pilot he'd trust more than Teacup. Through their years of flying together, they'd reached a level of communication where each knew what the other was thinking without any words spoken.

Now, across the airspace that separated them, Chance could see Teacup craning his head to look through the lower chin windows, before turning his aircraft in the direction of the attack.

"Nine o'clock, nine o'clock!" said Chance, but Fishhead was already pounding the hillside with a steady stream of fire from the 30 mm automatic cannon mounted beneath the fuselage.

"Mongo, complete delivery of package to Sangin. Over," Chance instructed the Black Hawk. Right now, their only mission was to ensure the safe delivery of the cleric. He watched as the Black Hawk and the second Apache wheeled away from the gunfire. Chance pushed forward on the collective, angling his own aircraft into a steep descent as he grimly surveyed the landscape beneath them.

"I see the bastards," Fishhead muttered, and gestured toward an outcropping of rock. As they swept overhead, Chance saw an ancient, covered truck. They were close enough to make out a group of men, dressed in local garb, pulling weapons out of the back. Without hesitating, Fishhead raked the area with gunfire. Several of the men fell, while others scrambled for cover on the rocky ground. Chance hovered over the site for an instant so he could get a fix on the truck. With a press of his finger, he deployed a Hellfire missile and watched in satisfaction as the entire area was obliterated.

A flash of light to his left caught his attention, and he looked in time to see two men with a shoulder launched missile taking aim at the other helicopters. The men had managed to scramble to a high vantage point several hundred feet from the site of the blast, and were in a perfect position to fire their weapon.

"Live MANPAD!" he shouted. "Incoming!" He depressed a button that launched a second Hellfire missile. In an instant, the spot where the two men had been standing was engulfed in a massive explosion, but not before the missile had been launched, screaming through the air directly toward the other two helicopters.

"Mongo, incoming! Deploy countermeasures!" Fishhead shouted into his headset.

Chance watched as the Apache released another round of diversionary flares, but even he could see the Black Hawk was flying too close.

"Mongo, pull up, pull up!" he shouted, and watched as the rocket exploded perilously close to the big helicopter. In that instant, he realized it could easily have been Jenna piloting that Black Hawk. Just the thought of her in this kind of danger made his stomach drop. Would she have been able to handle a combat situation? As a transport pilot, she'd probably never seen any hostile action, and although he knew she'd been upset about not being selected for this particular mission, he was thankful as hell that she was back at Kabul, where she was safe.

He watched in helpless astonishment now as debris from the missile exploded outward, striking the tail rotor of the Black Hawk and causing it to go into a dangerous spin. Their altitude was still high enough that unless McLaughlin regained control of the helicopter, the resulting crash would likely kill all souls aboard.

The Black Hawk yawed hard to the right and began to plummet downward, still spinning crazily. Without the tail rotor, the only thing McLaughlin could do was to try to keep the bird level. He might have a chance if he hit the ground on his wheels. The worst-case scenario would be if he tipped sideways and hit with his rotors. The force could tear the helicopter apart and spark an explosion.

"Sangin Ground, Alpha-Three-One-Six-Zero-Foxtrot, we have a Fallen Angel. Repeat, we have a Fallen Angel." He bit out the term used to signify a downed aircraft. "Request immediate ground support and medics. The area has been secured, over."

Even as he finished speaking, the Black Hawk hit the ground with a hard thud and, still spinning crazily, tipped forward, its rotors digging into the ground with enough force to send up a spray of dust and debris. The helicopter tipped onto its side and Chance saw the door gunner fall out and land on all fours, then pick himself up and scramble for safety, scant inches ahead of the deadly rotors. The helicopter careened wildly in a circle, sending chunks of rock and dirt flying into the air. Finally, it came to an abrupt stop, and Chance watched the gunner make his way back toward the wreckage.

"Alpha, I'm going down to lend assistance. Over." The radio transmission came from Teacup as he hovered over the crash site.

"Roger that, Teacup," Chance replied.

"Got you covered," Fishhead assured the other pilot.

They circled the area as the second Apache landed on the ground near the crash site, and Chance watched as the copilot climbed out of the cockpit and ran over to the wreckage. He kept an eye on the rescue mission, periodically searching the surrounding hills for any sign of further insurgency, but everything was quiet. Only the smoking ruins of the pickup truck and some burning brush gave any indication of the firefight. Below them, a convoy of armored vehicles left the forward operating base and made a beeline toward the downed Black Hawk, traveling fast.

Chance and Fishhead maintained a circular flight path around the wreckage site, alert to any signs of attack, until all of the crash victims had been extracted from the Black Hawk and loaded into the ground vehicles. Chance had no idea how serious the injuries were or if there had been any casualties, and that information would not be relayed over the radio, just in case their transmissions were being monitored.

Finally, the convoy of vehicles circled back toward the base and the second Apache lifted from the ground. The pilot gave Chance a thumbs-up, indicating there had been no fatalities, and they both flew in close formation over the convoy until it was safely behind the security perimeter of the base. Only after he and Teacup had performed one last check of the surrounding hills did they finally bring the birds in for a landing. Whether or not the military would retrieve the remains of the Black Hawk or destroy the aircraft altogether depended on the severity of damage sustained.

Once they had landed, a team of maintenance technicians descended on the Apaches to perform inspections and repairs. Chance walked over to where Teacup was talking with his copilot. He turned as Chance approached and extended his hand.

"That was some nice flying, T-Rex. And some damn nice shooting."

"Thanks. Did the package get delivered safely?"

Teacup nodded. "A few bumps and scratches, but otherwise okay. McLaughlin busted his arm and shoulder when the chopper tipped over, and his gunner is one lucky son of a bitch. If he was two seconds slower, he'd be toast. Sliced thin."

More than ever, Chance was glad that Jenna hadn't been part of this particular mission. If that had been her chopper that had taken the hit, or if she or one of her crew members had been injured… He knew men who'd quit flying for less. He glanced at his watch, anxious to be back in the air and on his return to Kabul. To Jenna. "Let's get the debrief over, so we can get back to Kabul."

"You actually think we're heading back there today?" Teacup's voice registered disbelief.

"Sure, why not? This should be an easy debrief. We were attacked and we responded to the threat." But even as he spoke the words, he knew he was kidding himself.

The other man's eyebrows went up. "I wish I could be that optimistic. We have a dozen or more dead insurgents, an injured pilot and crew, not to mention the other passengers on board, and an MH-60 that's badly damaged or a hunk of scrap metal." He made a scoffing sound. "This will cause a shit storm of paperwork and meetings. I wouldn't plan on going anywhere for at least a couple of days."

Teacup was right. Whenever there was a loss of life or aircraft, the resulting investigation could last for days, sometimes weeks. The forward operating base would want to send a team out to the hillside to inspect the area to try to determine who the insurgents were and if a threat still existed. Then there would be the endless debriefings and analysis of what had gone wrong and why they had failed to detect the threat earlier. The top brass would make every attempt to get him back into the air as quickly as possible, but it couldn't be soon enough for Chance.

He wanted to howl with frustration.

He'd promised Jenna that he would back at Kabul that night. If he was stuck at Sangin for the next couple of days, she would definitely be gone by the time he returned. No sandstorm lasted that long, and eventually her own command would insist upon her return. In fact, his own unit would feel the pinch of having two less Apaches at their disposal.

"Okay," he muttered, "let's get this done."

NIGHTFALL CAME QUICKLY in the desert, and even without the sandstorm, the darkness was nearly impenetrable. Jenna sat on her bed, propped up against her pillow and duffel bag, reading by a small light. But the words danced on the page and she couldn't focus on the narrative. She glanced at her wristwatch. Nearly seven o'clock, and still no sign of Chance. The team had departed ten hours ago; where the hell was he? He should have been back by now. Or maybe he'd returned and had decided not to come and see her. Either way, her insides were a jumble of nerves.

"Why don't you just go over to the operations shack and find out if they've returned," Laura suggested. "You've been sitting there, sighing and fidgeting, for over an hour, and quite frankly, it's driving me nuts."

Looking up, Jenna saw the other woman watching her. Their door gunner lounged on one of the bunks behind them, listening to music on her iPod, oblivious to their conversation. Giving up any pretense of reading, Jenna set the book aside and swung her legs over the edge of the bed, blowing out a hard breath. "I just have a bad feeling. What if something happened to him?"

Laura frowned. "What could happen? The guy's flying an Apache. He's virtually indestructible."

"What if the sandstorm caused a mechanical failure?"

"Just go over and find out, would you?"

At that moment, the door was flung open and Sergeant Melissa Robbins, their crew chief, stumbled inside. She closed the door behind her and then leaned against it, gasping for breath, her eyes wide behind her goggles. Seeing the expression on the other woman's face caused alarm to leap in Jenna's chest.

"What is it?" Her voice came out sharper than she intended.

"McLaughlin's chopper went down," the sergeant blurted. "Just outside Sangin. They were ambushed."

Someone gasped, and Jenna realized it was her. For just an instant, a wave of dizziness washed over her and her heartbeat thudded loud and insistent in her ears. It took a moment before she identified the sound as someone banging loudly on the door of the containerized housing unit. Galvanized into action, Jenna stood up and pulled the door open.

Chance stood there, a bandana covering his lower face and his eyes grim behind a pair of goggles. Relief caused her knees to go a little unsteady, and only the knowledge that the other women in the CHU were watching kept her from throwing herself into his arms.

"Can I come in?"

Jenna stepped back, opening the door wider, her gaze devouring him. She was only vaguely aware of her crew scrambling to their feet as they recognized the gold oak leaf on his uniform, signifying his rank as a major. Something wasn't right, though, and even as Jenna took in the special forces insignia on his sleeve, he removed his goggles and dragged the bandana away from his face, revealing a heavy growth of beard.

Chase!

Jenna gaped at Chance's twin brother, her stomach fisting in renewed fear.

"Chance is fine," he said without preamble, accurately reading her expression. "But they came under heavy fire just outside of Sangin. The MH-60 went down and McLaughlin was injured."

Relief at hearing Chance was okay drained the remaining strength out of Jenna's legs and she sat down heavily on the edge of her bunk. *At least it wasn't Chance who'd been injured.* Immediately, guilt washed over her at the unbidden thought. She might not like McLaughlin overly much, but she'd never wish him any harm. At the end of the day, he was still one of the good guys.

"Is McLaughlin going to be okay?"

"He's busted up some, but he'll live. They medevaced him to a coalition hospital at Kandahar and he'll be airlifted to Landstuhl in the morning. His aircraft won't be flying any more missions for a while, though."

Jenna gaped at him in horror. If McLaughlin was being airlifted to Landstuhl Hospital in Germany, then his injuries must be fairly serious. "What happened to him?"

"He'll need surgery on his shoulder and he sustained some internal injuries, but his prognosis for a full recovery is excellent. He'll be back in the air within six months, if not sooner." He looked at the female crew, who still stood behind her, listening, before his attention flicked back to her. "I came to tell you to head over to the operations shack. They need you to fly out to Sangin and pick up the rest of McLaughlin's crew and return them to Kandahar."

"Tonight?" Jenna couldn't keep the surprise out of her voice.

"No, first thing in the morning. The worst of the storm will have passed, although you'll be flying with poor visibility until the dust settles. Literally."

"Okay, I'll just grab my gear and head over."

"I'll wait."

Surprised, Jenna looked at him. "You don't need to do that. I can find my way."

"I'm sure you can, but I'm heading that way myself, so we may as well go together." His tone was polite but firm, and in that instant Jenna could see that his resemblance to Chance went more than skin deep.

"Okay, then," she murmured, and turned away to pull on her BDU jacket and grab her hat from the peg where it hung alongside her weapon. When Laura began grabbing her own gear, Jenna paused to give the other woman a questioning look.

"What?" Laura demanded. "You don't think you get to do this all by yourself, do you? I'm the copilot, so I'm going with you. That way I get to hear the report first hand and you don't need to repeat yourself."

Jenna gave her friend a brief smile, grateful for her support. "Thanks."

Outside, she was surprised to see a military vehicle waiting for them. An orange rotating light mounted on the roof cut through the thick, dark air. She slanted a speculative glance at Chase. He opened the door and hustled them in, before climbing in beside them.

"How'd you manage this?" she asked, removing her goggles. The flight ops shack was within walking distance of the housing area, and during brownout conditions, only emergency vehicles patrolled the streets of Kabul.

Chase shrugged and gave her a wry grin. "I have a few connections."

Jenna suspected that was an understatement. As an elite special forces commando, he probably had all kinds of connections. She was still struck by how much he looked like Chance, but despite the fact he was a gorgeous guy, she didn't feel the same tug of awareness that she did with his brother. In fact, she couldn't believe she'd thought he was Chance when she'd first seen him standing on her doorstep. Her only excuse was that he'd been wearing his goggles and bandana; had she been able to see his eyes clearly, she'd never have made that mistake.

Within minutes, they arrived at the operations shack, and Jenna saw the lights were still on in the briefing room. Now that she understood what was required of her, she was anxious to depart. She didn't want to wait until morning, but she knew the tac ops commander wouldn't allow her to fly at night during a sandstorm, no matter how experienced she might be.

Forty minutes later, after she and Laura had been briefed on the details of the ambush outside Sangin, she acknowledged that waiting until daybreak made sense. The insurgents would likely regroup after the morning's attack, and most ambushes and mortar attacks occurred during the night or bad weather, making a counter attack more difficult. Kabul had an Apache unit assigned to the base, and one of those aircraft would fly with her as an escort. Jenna had no doubt that she could handle whatever fate threw her way, but she was appreciative of the extra security.

Back at the CHU, she quickly briefed the rest of her

crew on the details of the next day's mission. If any of the women had misgivings about flying in brownout conditions into a combat area, they were too welltrained to show it. In fact, if Jenna wasn't mistaken, they actually looked eager to take on this assignment.

"Let's all get a good night's sleep, get our heads in the game and be ready to rock at oh-five-hundred hours," she suggested. But as she turned out the light and lay back on her narrow bunk, she wasn't thinking about the next day's mission. All she could think about was Chance and how grateful she was that he hadn't been injured, or worse, in the ambush. According to the tac ops commander, he'd been responsible for eliminating the threat, although the Apache's actions had come too late to prevent the Black Hawk from being hit.

Her father had flown dozens of combat missions, but he'd rarely talked about his experiences. Most of what Jenna knew of his career, she'd read in military and aviation magazines. She'd asked him about it once; whether he'd been scared when he'd flown his chopper into enemy territory to extract injured or trapped troops.

"Hell, yeah, I was scared," he'd answered. "Scared shitless. But it was also the most alive I've ever felt."

Jenna realized that's how she felt when she was with Chance. Just the thought of being in a serious relationship with him scared her out of her mind. But she'd never felt as alive as when they were together and his attention was focused solely on her. Could they possibly make a committed relationship work? She honestly didn't know.

Her parents' marriage had failed, partly because her father couldn't move past his days as a combat pilot. There was an exhilaration in flying that nothing else could match. Jenna understood that. She loved flying as much as her father did, but she didn't have an unrealistic expectation that everything in her life would be as exciting as sitting in the cockpit of an attack helicopter, not knowing if you'd return from a mission.

She'd sworn she'd never get involved with a pilot, but now she found herself wondering if a fellow pilot might not understand her better than a guy who had no military experience. If she and Chance decided to get serious, they'd have obstacles to overcome, but what couple didn't?

Turning on her side, she realized she was looking forward to the mission, and the possibility of seeing Chance at Sangin caused a thrill of anticipation to course through her. Just recalling their encounter in the cabin of the Black Hawk made her blood turn to honey in her veins. If he hadn't yet returned to Kabul, she'd tell him she wanted something more than just a casual relationship.

Did the thought scare her? Hell, yes, but it also made her feel alive. She suspected that she enjoyed being with Chance even more than she enjoyed flying.

11

CHANCE CIRCLED THE AREA where the insurgents had launched their attack the previous day, but nothing remained except a chunk of charred and twisted metal, the only evidence of what had once been a truck. It was just past nine o'clock in the morning, and he and Teacup had been flying for nearly two hours. But the sun was up and the sky was a little clearer than it had been the day before. Using both Apache aircraft, the two of them had been surveying the surrounding hills for almost an hour, searching for any further signs of hostility in the region.

He'd been told that two days earlier a marine infantry unit was dispatched to a region nearly sixty miles to the west. Local tribesmen had provided U.S. forces with information regarding a rural village located in the foothills, claiming it was actually a Taliban stronghold. Chance and Teacup had flown over the village but hadn't seen anything except farmers and goatherds. Not that that meant anything; the Taliban was notorious for blending in with the local population. There'd been no sign of the infantry unit, but that didn't worry Chance; they'd likely be traveling fast and light and would stay off the main roads. He'd spoken with his brother last night, after the attack, and Chase had told him that the unit had been preceded by a special operations team that would conduct reconnaissance and provide intel to the marines.

Now both pilots circled their helicopters back toward the base, satisfied that the region was safe. During their brief conversation, he'd also learned that Jenna would fly into Sangin that morning to transport McLaughlin's crew members back to Kandahar. He hated the thought of her at Sangin, which had seen more insurgency in the past few months than any other region in Afghanistan.

If it was up to Chance, he wouldn't have Jenna anywhere near this hellhole. She'd be back in the States, flying tourists around. He knew some would consider his attitude chauvinistic, but he didn't really care. He wanted her out of harm's way. If he was lucky, she'd be on the ground just long enough to load her passengers, and then she'd return to Kandahar. He desperately wanted to see her again, but he'd gladly sacrifice spending time with her if it meant she'd be safely away from this place.

He'd spent a sleepless night thinking about her, and in his dreams, he'd relived the attack. Only, instead of McLaughlin piloting the Black Hawk, it had been Jenna. He'd woken up with his heart pounding, disoriented and primed for battle, until he'd realized it had only been a nightmare. Now, in the light of morning, the dream seemed distant and vague, but his fear for Jenna's safety was still very real. He wouldn't let her suffer McLaughlin's fate because of a lack of vigilance on his part.

"T-Rex, everything looks clear. Suggest we return to base. Over."

Chance acknowledged that Teacup was right; they hadn't seen anything remotely suspicious, despite the fact they'd covered hundreds of square miles. He knew that Jenna was coming in with an Apache escort and there was no need for him to worry. She'd be okay.

"Roger that, Teacup," he responded, and angled the chopper back toward the base, watching as the shadow of his aircraft passed over the terrain beneath them. Despite his trepidation that the briefings regarding yesterday's attack would drag on forever, the officers in charge had quickly determined that both Chance and Captain Fuller had acted appropriately. The investigation into what happened to the Black Hawk would take longer, but all that mattered to Chance was that he'd been cleared to continue flying missions. And he'd already determined that his next one would be to escort Jenna's Black Hawk to Kandahar.

Flying in formation, they quickly covered the distance to Sangin. As they were cleared for landing and came in low across the outer perimeter, Chance saw two new helicopters sitting on the tarmac, a Black Hawk and an Apache, and he couldn't suppress the surge of adrenaline that had his heart pumping hard.

Jenna had arrived.

THE FLIGHT TO SANGIN had been uneventful, even when they'd been flying blind in the sandstorm. But as they'd drawn closer to the forward operating base, Jenna had found herself sitting straighter in the cockpit, her eyes scanning the landscape for any signs of a repeat ambush. She needn't have worried; both door gunners were on high alert, their machine guns trained on the rocks below. Laura had been in near constant communication with the base and they had been told that two

Apaches were performing a patrol of the area and that there had been no further signs of insurgency.

Without having to ask, Jenna had known that Chance was piloting one of those aircraft, and she'd felt a sense of calm as they'd traveled the last miles to the base. Now, as she completed her flight paperwork and climbed down from the cockpit, the *thwap-thwap* of helicopter rotors drew her attention skyward. Approaching from the west were two Apaches, and Jenna paused to watch them.

"Looks like your boyfriend is back," Laura murmured at her side, a knowing smile curving her mouth.

Jenna gave the other woman a warning look, but whatever she might have said was lost in the deafening sound of the rotor blades as the two helicopters descended to the tarmac beside them. Jenna threw up an arm to shield her face from the debris kicked up by the wash, but her heart leaped at the sight of the big birds. It didn't matter that she flew helicopters on a daily basis; she never got tired of watching them, and the distinctive sound of their engines and rotors never ceased to thrill her.

She looked through the dusty windshield of the nearest Apache and recognized Chance. Even the helmet and dark faceplate, reminiscent of Darth Vader, couldn't disguise the broad thrust of his shoulders or the way he held his head. When he turned in her direction, she knew he was looking at her. Then he reached up with both hands and removed the helmet, and their eyes met.

Jenna couldn't help herself. She smiled at him, happier to see him than she cared to admit, even to herself. She'd thought for sure that by the time she reached Sangin, he would already be on his way to rejoin his unit at Kabul Air Base in the north. That they were here, together, was more than she could have hoped for. Their stays could overlap for as little as an hour or for as long as several days, depending on the whims of the U.S. Military. She watched as he raised a finger to her in acknowledgment before returning his attention to his aircraft, shutting down the rotors and performing his postflight procedures. Giving herself a mental shake, Jenna turned her attention to her own aircraft and crew, but even as she went through the familiar motions, she was acutely aware of the man on the other side of the tarmac.

"This place is on high alert," hissed Laura. "I think our best bet is to round up McLaughlin's crew and get the hell out of Dodge."

Jenna glanced around. The flight line was a frenzy of activity as the ground maintenance crews descended on the helicopters and began performing the routine checks and inspections required to prepare the aircraft for their next mission. Beyond the tarmac, military vehicles rumbled along the dusty roads, lights flashing on their roofs. Groups of soldiers walked with their weapons in the ready position as they performed security patrols throughout the base. Guards manned the towers along the perimeter wall, using high-optic binoculars to peer over the sandbags and razor-wire barriers into the surrounding desert.

Jenna knew Laura was right; they should just collect their cargo and continue on to Kandahar, but there was an excitement in the air—a sort of energy—that appealed to her, despite the inherent danger. She'd never had to fly in an active combat environment, and realistically she knew she shouldn't want to, but for just an instant she envied Chance his position as an Apache fighter pilot. If it came time to engage the enemy, nobody would question his right to be there or his ability to handle the situation. Even though she manned a Black Hawk helicopter, armed with some of the most lethal weapons in the U.S. arsenal, there would be those who would question her skills or whether she should even be allowed to fly such a mission, simply because she was female.

"Hey, you okay?"

Jenna turned and found herself staring into Chance's light green eyes. His cropped hair was damp from his helmet, and sweat coated the strong column of his throat above the collar of his flight suit. Lines of fatigue were visible on his face, but his eyes were alight with pleasure as they raked over her.

"Chance." Was that her voice that sounded so breathless?

"No problems coming in?" he asked, running a critical eye over her aircraft, as if he expected to see bullet holes in the fuselage.

"None," she assured him. "The flight was uneventful."

"Good." Glancing around, he caught her by the elbow and drew her toward the operations shack. "Listen, I'm glad you're here and I wish I could spend some time with you, but—"

Jenna pulled her arm free, annoyed, because she *had* hoped to spend some time with him while she was at Sangin, and his words felt like a rejection.

"We both need to stay focused," he continued, falling into step beside her. "There'll be a time and place for us to be together but, trust me, this isn't it."

Jenna gave a soft, disbelieving laugh and shook her head. The fact that he was completely focused on the mission, while she'd been daydreaming about another encounter with him, filled her with self-loathing. When had she become such a bimbo?

"I'm not here for a social visit," she said stiffly, knowing she must sound like a total bitch. "I'm here to do a job."

"That's not what I meant," he said in a low voice, his brow furrowing at her tone. "I'd hoped that we'd have some time to just hang out together, and maybe we still can, but intel has reports of more insurgency about sixty miles to the west. I think you should collect up Mongo's crew and head out as soon as you can. I'd feel better if you were back at Kandahar. That's all I'm saying."

Jenna came to an abrupt stop and whirled on him. "What's that supposed to mean?"

"Jesus," he bit out, scrubbing a hand over his hair. "Can't a guy express concern for your well-being without you taking it the wrong way?"

Jenna bit back a sharp retort and looked swiftly out over the tarmac, trying to contain her emotions. She was being unfair, especially when he seemed genuinely concerned about her.

"Listen," she said quietly. "I understand why you want me gone, but this is my job. It's what I do, the same as you. I know I don't have any real combat experience, but I can handle whatever comes my way. I've been trained for this, Chance. Please don't doubt my abilities."

For the first time, Jenna saw real anger flare in his eyes.

"Is that what you think?" he asked softly, his tone registering his dismay. "Because if you do, then you don't know the first thing about me. I've never questioned your capabilities as a pilot. I'm sure you can handle whatever the mission requires. I don't want you *gone*. I want you *safe*." He blew out a hard breath and looked away for a moment, clearly trying to rein in his emotions. When he finally turned back to her, his expression was controlled and shuttered. "You know what? Maybe you're right. Maybe this thing between us won't work."

His words cut through her like a blade, but there was no way she'd let him see that. Instead, she made a scoffing noise. "There's a reason I don't get involved with other pilots, and you've just proven my point. You said it yourself—we need to stay focused. I'm here to do a job, and if that job requires me to fly into a combat situation, then I will."

Seeing the frustration on his face, Jenna felt herself soften, just a bit. "Listen, I knew exactly what I was getting into when I joined the military. I knew it wouldn't all be training exercises and flying dignitaries around the country. I understood that *this*—" she gestured to the surrounding base, with its concrete barriers and concertina wire "—would also be part of the job. I'm okay with it, and you should be, too. And if you're not…"

She left the words unspoken, but they hung in the air between them. If he wasn't okay with it, then there really wasn't much point in pursuing any kind of relationship. He needed to see her as an equal, because she wouldn't agree to anything else.

"I'll accept it," he finally said, grudgingly, "but that doesn't mean I have to like it."

Jenna slanted him a sidelong glance, wishing he didn't look so good in his flight suit. Even the bulky body armor and survival vest he wore did little to detract from his physique.

"When do you return to Kabul?" she asked, her annoyance quickly evaporating as she saw how weary he was. She reminded herself that it could just as easily have been his chopper that went down, and a cold fist clutched at her heart. She'd known him for such a short time, but she didn't know what she'd do if anything happened to him. If that was how he'd felt when he thought of her flying a combat mission, then she could easily forgive him.

"Given yesterday's incident, Teacup and I will stick around for a day or two until the initial investigation is complete. We'll do another flyover of the area this afternoon."

Jenna nodded. Both foot patrols and a strong air presence were a vital part of any counterinsurgency effort.

Chance glanced at his watch. "It's barely nine-thirty. Feeling hungry?"

"Yes, actually, I am." She looked over her shoulder to see if Laura would join them, but she was standing by the helicopter, talking with one of the other copilots. "Give me thirty minutes, okay? I need to check in with tac ops, and I want to see how McLaughlin's crew is doing. Meet me by the operations shack in a half hour?"

"I'm headed that way myself," he responded smoothly, "so let's just go together, okay?"

His words were completely plausible, since he had just returned from a mission and would need to debrief with the tac ops commander, yet Jenna couldn't shake the sense that he didn't intend to let her out of his sight. Normally, that kind of scrutiny would annoy her and she'd insist on going separately, so she was unprepared for the surge of pleasure she felt. She didn't say anything, just continued walking, but she couldn't quite suppress the small smile that tugged at the corners of her mouth.

Jenna waited in the flight ops shack while Chance debriefed his commanding officers about the morning's mission. Laura and the other pilots had drifted into the shack behind her as she completed her own paperwork for the flight from Kabul. Now they listened as the tac ops commander briefed them on the security situation outside the base. The special ops team, a group of army rangers, had reached a ridge several klicks west of the rural village. They were actively watching the activities of the villagers, but were unable to positively identify any Taliban presence.

There was silence in the small room for a moment, and Jenna glanced at the faces around her. She knew they were all thinking about the previous day's attack on the Black Hawk helicopter. The Taliban was out there, and it was only a matter of time before the U.S. troops tracked them down and eliminated them. The knowledge that she would not be part of that mission rankled just a little. As much as she understood the importance of flying Captain McLaughlin's crew back to Kandahar so they could return to duty, she couldn't help but wish she could be assigned to a mission where she could make a real difference.

As if he'd read her thoughts, the tac ops commander flipped a page on his clipboard and looked directly at her.

"Captain Larson, welcome to Sangin. Our one med-evac chopper was required to evacuate a casualty to Kandahar earlier this morning and isn't expected back until later tonight. Therefore, you and your crew will remain on site as backup until they return. You'll stay in B-Hut Eleven-Foxtrot tonight. I have you cleared for departure tomorrow at oh-eight-hundred hours."

Jenna had been so sure that she would depart that very day for Kandahar that it took a moment to realize she would stay the night at Sangin. The tac ops commander was an older man with deep creases on his face, and now he waited for Jenna's acknowledgment.

"Is that acceptable to you, Captain Larson?" he asked, a ghost of a smile touching his lips.

"Absolutely," she responded quickly.

She forced herself to concentrate on the commander, when what she really wanted to do was look over at Chance to see his response to this news. He'd said earlier that he would make one more sweep of the area that afternoon, but he hadn't indicated whether he would return to Kabul Airbase immediately, or if he would also remain at Sangin. As forward operating bases went, Sangin wasn't the worst place to be assigned, but it lacked the amenities of the larger bases. This was a true combat support base.

The briefing over, Jenna hung back while the other pilots left, until just she and Chance remained.

"How about some breakfast?" he asked.

Jenna grimaced, adjusting her weapon to a more comfortable position in its leather holster. Her body armor weighed a ton, and even this early in the morning, the heat was oppressive. Beneath her flight suit, sweat trickled between her breasts and her hair felt heavy and sticky.

"How about an ice-cold beer and a lounge chair next to a swimming pool?" she muttered.

He grinned, and Jenna couldn't help staring at him. The man was breathtaking when he smiled, the deep dimples in his lean cheeks drawing a reluctant smile from her. "Will you settle for a cold O.J. and an air-conditioned mess hall? I have a couple of hours before I need to be back here."

Jenna knew he referred to the reconnaissance mission he would fly that afternoon. They left the operations shack and went to the chow hall. With his flight suit and sunglasses, and his easy loose-limbed stride, Chance drew his fair share of appreciative glances from the female soldiers they passed, and Jenna felt a rush of possessive pride that he was walking with *her*.

The mess hall was small, but the food was plentiful and looked fresh. They chose a table near the wall, and she tried not to stare at the astonishing amount of food that Chance had mounded on his plate.

"How do you not gain weight, eating all that?" she asked.

He shrugged and tucked in. "A high metabolism, I guess." He indicated the yogurt and fruit she'd chosen for herself. "How do you stay alive eating just that?"

Jenna looked ruefully at her meager breakfast. "I have to watch what I eat or I won't fit into the cockpit."

Chance's eyes turned hot as he studied her. "You don't have to watch what you eat, trust me. With your height, you could actually stand to put on a few pounds. Not that I'm complaining." His voice dropped to a sexy growl. "I think you look amazing."

Her entire life, people had commented on her height or made jokes about how tall she was. Whenever she'd been inclined to slouch, her father had barked at her to stand straight, stand tall. Every summer, he'd mark her growth on a piece of trim board in his kitchen, grunting each time the pencil mark moved higher. But it wasn't until she'd become a commissioned officer that he'd commented directly on her stature.

"My dad once told me that the only advantage my height would give me was the ability to look a man straight in the eye when I gave him an order." She arched an eyebrow at him. "Maybe I should try that with you. What do you think? Would you be duly intimidated into obeying me?"

Chance's eyes gleamed. "I guess that depends. I still have a few inches on you, but I seem to recall at least one instance when we were on perfect eye level with each other."

Jenna knew he referred to their encounter in the Black Hawk, when she had straddled his thighs, her feet easily reaching the ground as she levered herself over him. Yeah, they'd been at perfect eye level. The memory caused her breath to catch, and when Chance's gaze fastened on her mouth, Jenna felt a tightening in her abdomen and a rush of heat between her legs.

She cleared her throat and glanced around, hoping nobody noticed the electricity that seemed to leap between them. The small chow hall was busy, even at midmorning, with soldiers and some contractor civilians, but no one paid any attention to her and Chance. Dropping her gaze, Jenna pushed her yogurt around with her spoon, her appetite for food gone. What she wanted now couldn't be satisfied by eating.

"Funny how a day can change everything," she murmured. "Right now, Kabul Airbase seems like a lifetime ago."

"Not to me," Chance said quietly. "When I was turning in last night, I could have sworn I smelled your scent on my skin."

For a long moment, their gazes locked and held, and

Jenna forgot to breathe. A tray clattered nearby, breaking the spell and snapping her attention away from the mesmerizing expression in his light green eyes.

"So when do you leave?" she asked, focusing on her yogurt and fruit. She didn't dare look at him again, in case he saw how much his words affected her. She wouldn't admit it to him, but she'd found herself replaying those moments in the Black Hawk over and over again in her mind more times than she cared to admit.

"Teacup and I will fly a reconnaissance mission to the west in a few hours. We'll bunk here tonight before we head back to Kabul in the morning." He leaned across the table toward her, his lips compressed in a clear sign of frustration. "I was really hoping we could find some time alone, but that could be a little difficult with both of us staying in B-Huts."

B-Huts were open sleeping quarters, usually contained inside a large tent, with as many as thirty or more soldiers sleeping side by side on narrow cots. On a base as remote as Sangin, B-Huts were the norm. As commissioned officers, she and Chance should have been assigned to a CHU, but Sangin was too small for such luxuries.

Jenna shrugged, forcing a nonchalance she was far from feeling. "It's okay. Even if we had our own CHUs, it's not like we could visit each other."

General Order No. 1 prohibited soldiers from entering the sleeping quarters of the opposite sex, and violations were dealt with severely. As much as Jenna might want Chance, she wouldn't risk a reprimand, or worse, simply because she couldn't keep a lid on her libido.

Chance sighed and sat back in his chair, rubbing a hand across his eyes. "Jesus, I'd give anything to be at Kandahar or Kabul right now." When he lowered his hand, his expression was an alluring combination of awareness and frustration. Knowing that he wanted her was almost enough to make up for the fact that they couldn't be together.

"Maybe they're showing a movie over at the rec center tonight," she suggested. "We could check that out."

"What…like a date?"

Jenna heard the gentle teasing in his voice and recalled their conversation from the previous day regarding the status of their relationship. She'd been clear that she didn't want anyone in her unit knowing about them. But with McLaughlin's crew stranded at Sangin, there was a distinct likelihood they would see her with Chance and draw their own conclusions.

Suddenly, she didn't care. If there was one thing she'd realized in the past twenty-four hours, it was that life was short and you had to grab what you wanted with both hands. And right now she wanted Chance Rawlins. She'd been an army pilot for eight years; people would start to talk if she didn't show interest in someone as overtly sexy as Chance Rawlins.

She looked at him from beneath her lashes and allowed a small smile to curve her lips. "Yeah, just like a date."

Chance laced his hands across his flat stomach and regarded her lazily. "Only, there's no chance of my stealing a kiss or copping a feel."

Jenna laughed. "Sorry, none. Unless of course…"

He arched an eyebrow and waited.

"Unless you choose to walk me back to my sleeping quarters. We could take the long way around. Maybe go over to the flight line and check on my aircraft."

Chance's expression grew heated. "There's no sand-storm. We could be seen."

"I'll risk it." Just thinking about being with him again caused butterflies of excitement to flutter in her stomach. She didn't want to wait. She felt as if she'd been stretched taut, and if she didn't get some relief, she would snap. "Do you want to get out of here?"

"Sweetheart," he drawled, devouring her with his eyes, "if I stand up now, every soldier in this canteen is going to know I'm having indecent thoughts about you."

"Oh." Only then did she realize he'd placed his hat across his lap to hide his growing arousal. *"Oh."*

"Let's talk about something else," he suggested. "How did you come to have an all-female crew?"

Jenna shook her head. "I don't know. It just sort of worked out that way. I met Laura—Warrant Officer Costanza—at flight school and then we happened to get assigned to the same unit. We work really well together. If she wasn't my copilot, I'd want her as my wingman. I guess I've never really thought of us as an all-female crew. We're professionals who're just doing our jobs."

"So you'd have no problem flying with a male copilot? Or copiloting for a male pilot?"

"Absolutely not. In fact, I've done both. Would you object to flying with a female copilot? Or copiloting for a female pilot?"

"I've never really thought about it," he admitted. "But as long as she knew her stuff and could get the job done, then no, I'd have no objections."

"You don't think there'd be any underlying resent-ment, or a need to prove yourself?"

Chance leaned forward and looked directly into her eyes. "No. I. Don't."

Jenna was unconvinced. "You can say that now because you've never been in that situation."

Chance looked affronted. "How do you know?"

"Well, have you?" Jenna would stake her life on the fact that Chance had never had to fly with a female copilot, which was why he was able to dismiss her fears about getting involved with another pilot as rubbish.

"Yes, actually," he replied smoothly. "I flew four missions with a female gunner during my last deployment, when my own copilot had to undergo an emergency appendectomy."

Jenna didn't know why that information should surprise her so much, but it did. At the same time, she was aware of a niggling sense of jealousy at the thought of another woman riding shotgun with Chance, working in tandem with him and anticipating his needs and commands.

"That surprises you," he said flatly, reading her expression.

"Frankly, yes."

"Why? Because you were more comfortable thinking of me as a—how did you so eloquently put it? A shallow, narcissistic, egotistical, arrogant pilot, with all the stereotypical chauvinistic attitudes?"

Jenna frowned, because whether she wanted to admit it or not, his words had a ring of truth. She *had* wanted to think of him that way, so that when their relationship came to its inevitable end, she could put the blame squarely on him.

"Look," she said carefully. "I may have been wrong about you, okay?"

Chance's eyebrows shot up. "Wow. That sounds suspiciously like an apology."

Jenna gave him a rueful look, but her heart was

pounding hard in her chest. She was going to step out on a limb and hope it didn't snap beneath her. If someone had told her just two months ago that she would be willing to get emotionally involved with another pilot, she would never have believed it. She could scarcely believe it now, and even though her head was telling her that she was about to make a colossal mistake, everything else—body, heart and soul—were telling her that this was what she wanted.

"I guess what I'm trying to say is that I'm willing to give this—this *relationship* a try."

She waited breathlessly for his response. She'd thought he would be happy, but he merely gave her a skeptical look. "What about your conditions? You know, keeping it casual?"

Jenna looked at him sharply. "Is that what you want?"

He raised his hands and sat back in his chair. "Don't turn this around on me, sweetheart. I told you how I feel, but I'm willing to play this however you want. If you don't want me to talk to you in front of your unit, then I need to know that."

Jenna drew in a deep breath. "I guess what I'm trying to say is that we don't have to keep it under wraps. We may be restricted from public displays of affection, but that doesn't mean we can't be seen together. Even by the guys in my unit."

Chance's mouth lifted in a lopsided grin. "I'm going to hold you to that."

"You don't trust me? How are we going to make any kind of relationship work if you don't trust me?"

Her words had been partly teasing, but his were serious as he considered her. After a long moment, he pushed his chair back and rose to his feet. "I'm going to tell you the same thing a pilot told me the first time I flew as a copilot, and it's the same thing I've told each copilot who's climbed into the cockpit with me—first and foremost, we're equals. Every time we undertake a mission together, risks are identified and mitigated when possible. Each of us is charged with constantly monitoring the mission and re-evaluating the risks, and each of us has a voice in the mission and is charged with speaking up if concerns arise."

Jenna knew he wasn't just talking about flying. "Okay. I'm in total agreement with you."

Chance braced his hands on the table and leaned forward to look at her, his face scant inches from her own. "But none of that undermines the authority of whoever is in control, and that person will always have the final say."

Jenna's heart thumped hard in her chest, but she returned his gaze steadily. "And which one of us is in control?"

She was unprepared when he reached out and stroked a thumb across her mouth. His expression was one of amused resignation. "Well, it sure as hell isn't me, sweetheart."

12

"MAN, WHO PICKED THIS movie? This is seriously lame."

Jenna leaned forward on the sofa and gave the speaker a level look. "I did. This is only one of the best movies ever made."

Sergeant Byron Jones made a scoffing noise. He was Captain McLaughlin's door gunner and he and Jenna had known each other for several years.

"Aw, c'mon, Captain L., get real. What's so great about an old dude reading a book to some old lady in a nursing home?"

"It's a romance, Jones," interjected another crew member, Corporal Matt Logan. "You're gonna love it. This movie is right up your alley—all mushy and sentimental."

Byron gave the other man a look of disgust. "Man, I'm gonna hit you with something really hard. What the hell are you doin', bro?"

"Busting your balls." Corporal Logan grinned unrepentantly.

"If it makes you feel any better, Jones," said Laura from where she sat cross-legged on the floor with her back against the wall, "I promise not to notice if you cry."

Beside her on the sofa, Chance shifted restlessly and stretched his long legs out in front of him. He had returned from his afternoon mission just an hour earlier and had just completed his flight briefing with the ops commander. Jenna hadn't had a chance to ask him how the mission had gone, but his expression seemed a little on the grim side. They had agreed to meet at the recreation center at seven o'clock to watch a movie, but Jenna hadn't been prepared to find Captain McLaughlin's entire crew there, as well as her own. She'd hoped that she and Chance might have the place to themselves, but no such luck.

Out of deference to her rank and, she suspected, her gender, she had been invited to choose the movie. The selection of DVDs ran mostly to action and suspense flicks, but Jenna had taken a perverse pleasure in choosing a film that critics called an epic love story.

The recreation center was no more than a rough, plywood structure with a couple of worn sofas and chairs inside, but it also boasted a large, flat-screen television and a decent surround-sound system. On the far side of the room were two additional televisions and a couple of video-game consoles, where a group of young soldiers enthusiastically played a warfare game, as if they didn't get enough of it in real life.

Jenna sat next to Chance on the sofa, while the other crew members sprawled on the scattered chairs or sat on the floor. The air-conditioning whirred softly, and Jenna welcomed the cool air against her skin. Like most of the other soldiers, she wore a T-shirt and her camo pants, but had left her jacket and body armor in the B-Hut that she would share with twenty other women.

The soldiers had each brought their weapon with them, and they lay on the floor by the entrance. Someone had made popcorn, and as the bowl was passed around, Jenna felt like she might actually be able to relax and enjoy the downtime.

Chance stretched an arm along the sofa behind her head, and she froze, acutely aware of him. Her thigh pressed against his, and her shoulder fit neatly into the curve of his arm. She realized she could smell him, a clean scent of soap and spicy deodorant. His chest rose and fell evenly with his breathing, and she wondered if he was as aware of her as she was of him. But when Laura unfolded herself from the floor and stood up to flick the lights off, Jenna's awareness ratcheted up to a whole new level.

"Sorry," said Laura, sounding anything but apologetic. "That overhead light hurts my eyes and causes a glare on the screen."

There were murmured assents, and when Laura returned to her seat, Chance bent his head to whisper softly in her ear. "Well this is cozy. Maybe I can cop a feel after all."

Jenna didn't dare look at him. "I wouldn't advise it," she whispered back, knowing he wouldn't make good on his threat, at least not here. Instead, he traced his thumb lazily over the back of her shoulder, where none of the others could see. That small contact made her feel connected to him in a way that even having sex with him hadn't.

When an explicit love scene played out in the movie, several of the soldiers squirmed uncomfortably or made crude jokes in an attempt to alleviate the tension that filled the small room. Jenna watched, imagining that the characters making love on the floor were her and

Chance. As if he could read her thoughts, he stroked her bare arm with his fingertips, the featherlight caress causing goose bumps of sensation to rise on her skin.

"That's what I want to do to you," he breathed.

Jenna felt something loosen in her chest, but when she looked at him, his attention was still fixed on the television screen, and the shifting light cast shadows over his taut features. Without turning his head, he looked at her, and the heat in his eyes caused an internal meltdown as her body responded to the implicit promise in his eyes.

The intimacy of the moment was shattered by a strident alarm. The warning sirens that blared through the compound had every person in the rec center, including Jenna and Chance, leaping to their feet and scrambling for their weapons, the movie forgotten. Each one of them knew what the sirens meant: an incoming rocket or mortar attack.

"Bunkers!" yelled Sergeant Jones, springing forward to throw the door open and hustle everyone through.

Jenna paused long enough to grab her pistol and holster off the floor before she dashed outside. Theoretically, the sirens were supposed to provide a ten- to twenty-second advance warning, but the first explosion came just five seconds after the first alarm sounded. Too late, she realized she had neither helmet nor body armor. Until she reached the safety of the bunker, she was completely vulnerable.

Outside, darkness had fallen. As she sprinted out the door, Jenna looked up into the sky and came to an abrupt halt, heedless of the person who plowed into her from behind. She stared in amazement at the unbelievable sight of a rocket whizzing directly overhead, followed an instant later by an explosion that made the ground tremble beneath her feet. Another rocket whistled above her and she could have sworn it was no more than thirty feet from the ground, but this time it was intercepted by an anti-missile system and exploded in midair.

"Larson," growled a voice behind her, "move your ass!"

Before she could respond, Chance wrapped a hand around her arm, almost dragging her alongside as they ran toward the nearest bunker. Overhead, red tracers crisscrossed the night sky, and another explosion rocked the compound. It was like a scene from *Star Wars,* as laser cannons blasted away in retaliation and the sound of machine-gun fire filled the air.

Then they were in the bunker, stumbling their way down the incline and into the cool darkness of the fortified dugout. The sounds of the rockets were muffled here, but the explosions illuminated the interior in brief, ghostly flashes of light. More than two dozen other soldiers were there ahead of them, standing silently as they waited for the attack to end.

Chance pulled Jenna into a corner and, heedless of anyone who might be watching, caught her face in his hands, searching her eyes in the gloom.

"You okay?"

"Yes." Now that they were safely in the bunker, she realized that she was shaking. The attack was the closest she'd come to real combat, and as much as the rockets had mesmerized her, they had also scared her.

"Where the hell is your helmet and vest?" Chance asked, his voice tight.

"Where are yours?" she countered breathlessly, taking in his T-shirt and camo pants.

"Christ." He scrubbed a hand over his face. "I know better. We both know better."

Neither of them had brought any protective gear with them to the rec center, and Jenna realized the oversight could have cost them their lives. Even in the indistinct light, she could see how much the personal security lapse bothered him.

"Hey," she said, laying a hand on his arm. "We're okay. We made it to the bunker. Everything is okay." At that moment, she became aware that the sirens had stopped, and the others were making their way cautiously outside. The sound of rockets had ceased. "Listen! It's over."

But Chance wasn't listening. He thrust Jenna up against the cold concrete blocks of the bunker wall, searching her eyes in the darkness. There was an edge to him that Jenna hadn't seen before, a desperation of sorts.

"You don't understand," he persisted grimly. "We knew there was the possibility of an attack. *I* knew this was a possibility. We lost an aircraft yesterday and yet here we are, running around without any protective gear like we're at a damned *resort.*"

"Chance, we're okay," Jenna said fiercely. "I'm okay."

She heard him draw in a deep, steadying breath, and then he slid his hands up her arms until he cradled her jaw in his palms. "I was afraid for you," he said simply. And then he bent his head and covered her mouth with his own.

HE FELT JENNA STIFFEN IN surprise, and he couldn't blame her. There was nothing remotely gentle or romantic about the kiss. In fact, it felt a little bit like an all-out assault, yet he was helpless to use any restraint. He hadn't been kidding when he'd told Jenna that she had all the control. Right now, his own was T-minus and counting.

When the rockets had started coming in, his first thought had been for Jenna and he'd been right behind her as she'd made a dash for the bunker. But when she'd stopped to watch the fireworks, he'd had an instant of pure terror that one of those damned things was going to explode too close and either kill her outright or seriously injure her.

Slowly, he became aware that Jenna had relaxed under his hands and was leaning into him. Her hands clutched his back and she was returning his kiss with the same passion and intensity that he was putting into it. She made a sound of approval and some of the raw fear in his gut dissipated. He gentled the kiss, angling his mouth over hers as he explored her with his tongue. She tasted faintly of the red licorice that Laura had shared with her during the movie and he wanted to eat her.

Jenna broke the contact first, pulling back and pressing her lips together as if she would hold on to the taste of him. Chance dragged air into his lungs and braced a hand on the wall behind her head.

"Sorry," he muttered. "I didn't mean to do that."

Her hands smoothed over the front of his T-shirt as if she would soothe him. "No, don't apologize. I wanted you to kiss me. I've wanted you to kiss me since I first arrived this morning."

He raised his head, about to tell her how he felt, but before he could form the words, they were interrupted by a shadow blocking the entrance to the bunker.

"Major Rawlins?"

Chance recognized the voice of his gunner and copilot, Warrant Officer Harrell. He straightened, moving away from Jenna.

"What is it, Fishhead?"

"You're wanted over at the operations shack."

"Thanks, I'll be right there."

"Uh, sir?" Fishhead hesitated. "Captain Larson is wanted there, too."

Chance glanced at Jenna, and his chest tightened. There was only one reason why they would both be summoned to the operations shack, and it had nothing to do with their extracurricular activities.

"They're putting together a counterattack," Jenna breathed.

Chance knew she was right but, damn it, did she have to sound so excited? He mentally braced himself as he followed her out of the bunker and across the small base to the flight ops shack. The likelihood of Jenna flying a combat mission against the insurgents was slim to none; she was a transport pilot. She had virtually no experience working in a combat environment, and the top brass knew that. There was no way they'd assign her to such a dangerous mission. Still, he couldn't quite tamp down the sense of foreboding he felt.

Although the 170mm rockets no longer whizzed overhead, and the warning sirens and laser cannons were now silent, the compound was anything but quiet as troops and military vehicles made their way through the dusty streets. By the time they reached the flight ops shack, the crew members of all three Apaches and Jenna's aircraft were already there.

"We have a situation," Colonel Tyler, their commander, said without preamble, and indicated an area on the large map of the Helmand region behind him.

He quickly explained that the insurgents responsible for the rocket attack had been located, and a nearby marine unit had closed in on the location and engaged the enemy.

"The soldiers have been pinned down by heavy Taliban fire with one soldier badly wounded. My medevac chopper is enroute from Kandahar, but won't arrive for another forty minutes," the commander stated. "We've requested air support from Camp Leatherneck, but we can be on site faster than any other responder. I have a flight surgeon ready to go. Who are my pilots?"

"I'll fly," Jenna said quickly, stepping forward. "My helo is ready and my crew and I can be in the air in five minutes."

Chance wanted to drag her back and clap his hand over her mouth to prevent the words from being spoken, but it was too late. He'd known before the commander finished talking that Jenna would volunteer for the mission. There was a part of him that wanted to protest that she had no practical combat experience, but he knew she would never forgive him if he did. She might not be combat-tested, but he reminded himself that this was what she had been trained to do. She was an experienced pilot. He couldn't prevent her from going out there, but he could at least ensure she didn't get herself killed.

"I'll provide cover." He made it a statement, wanting it clear that his participation wasn't negotiable. "Teacup and I are familiar with the territory."

Colonel Tyler nodded. "Five minutes and I want those birds in the air. This is the golden hour, troops, if we want to save that man's life. Let's go, and God bless."

Chance knew he referred to the brief window of time

in which a critically injured trauma patient could be saved, provided he had medical treatment. It was up to them to ensure the injured soldier received that treatment. This was just one reason why Chance was proud to wear his uniform; the military didn't hold back on efforts to retrieve wounded soldiers, no matter how low the soldier's rank or how high the risk.

They left the ops shack at a dead run, making a beeline for the flight line. Chance fell into step beside Jenna.

"I'll be right there, laying down fire. If you begin taking fire, I want you to haul ass out of there, got it?" He gave her his best "that's an order" look, but Jenna barely glanced at him.

"I'll do whatever it takes to get that man out," she replied.

They had reached the helicopters, where the ground crews had already fired up the engines and had their flight gear waiting for them. The troop seats had been removed from the Black Hawk cabin, leaving a clean configuration that allowed room for several stretchers. The flight surgeon and two medics were in the process of loading their lifesaving equipment into the open space, assisted by the crew chief and several ground-crew members. Jenna paused long enough to pull on her harness and survival vest, and Chance took precious seconds to drive his point home.

"I'm serious, Jenna," he said fiercely. "Don't pull any heroics, okay? We can't risk losing an entire crew and an aircraft just because you want to prove yourself. You're not your father."

Jenna did look at him then, and her eyes flashed with a mixture of anger and disbelief. "I can't believe you just said that. Is that what you really think?" she hissed. "That I volunteered for this mission because I have something to prove? If so, then you don't know the first thing about me. I'm going up there, and I'm going to do *my job,* Major." She gave him one all-encompassing, scathing look. "I suggest you do the same."

She turned and climbed into the cockpit without another word, and Chance barely resisted the urge to drag her back. He'd never felt so helpless, and he knew that even if they both survived the rescue mission and returned to Sangin, he may have already lost her.

13

As the Black Hawk lifted Jenna forced herself to put Chance and his parting words out of her mind. She needed to get her head in the game and focus on the mission. Checking the coordinates on her display, she saw they would reach the extraction point in less than seven minutes.

Beside her, Laura monitored the radio, and in the cabin behind her, she could hear the flight surgeon and the two medics setting up their equipment. The Black Hawk was not a medevac helicopter and had not been modified for medical evacuation, like the DUSTOFF Black Hawks, which were used exclusively as air ambulances. But the medics had brought their own portable lifesaving supplies and equipment and were rapidly converting the cabin into a triage center.

The blackness of the surrounding desert was total, forcing both pilots to wear night-vision goggles. The monochromatic green landscape lent an eerie, surreal quality to the mission. Glancing out her left window, Jenna could see an Apache flying just above her and knew it was Chance. From her vantage point, she didn't have a visual on the second Apache, piloted by Teacup, but knew it was flanking her right side.

Laura had made contact with the Joint Terminal Attack Controller, the soldier on the ground responsible for maintaining radio contact with the air-support crews and providing real-time information regarding their situation. Jenna listened as the JTAC provided the coordinates for a safe location in which to land so they could evacuate the wounded soldier.

Looking at the map on the display, Jenna realized it would be a tricky maneuver. The troops were pinned down in a heavily wooded area with a river behind them and enemy fire coming at them from a ridge on the other side of a clearing. The ideal situation would be to land in the open space, but the Apache helicopters would need to lay down a significant amount of suppressive fire to keep the insurgents from attacking them. Even if they were able to do that, the ground troops would need to transport the injured soldier more than two hundred yards to the clearing.

"We'll keep the sons of bitches on the ridge occupied," Chance said through her headset. "Goalie, it's your game."

True to his word, the two Apaches swept in low over the ridge and proceeded to hammer the site with cannon fire. At the same time, Jenna wheeled the Black Hawk toward the clearing, keeping as close to the trees as possible in order not to expose the injured soldier to enemy fire. But as she hovered over the landing site and prepared to descend, a burst of small-arms fire peppered the ground below. *Ping! Ping!* Something hit the side of the helicopter in a metallic staccato.

"We're taking fire," Laura barked into the headset. "Climb! Climb!"

Jenna pulled back on the cyclic stick until she was more than sixty feet above the trees.

"The attack came from the south side of the clearing," her door gunner called. "That puts the extraction site in a direct cross fire with the ridge."

"T-Rex, sweep the south side of the clearing," Jenna directed, swinging the Black Hawk back around so that she was above the clearing once again and facing whatever threat might come from the south. As she watched, an Apache rocketed through the night and she could see the tracers from the rockets as Chance pounded the region. "JTAC, we're going to try again."

"That's a negative," came the reply. "We cannot move the casualty. Repeat, we are unable to move our man to the landing zone."

Jenna exchanged a meaningful look with Laura. The injury must be bad if they couldn't risk moving him two hundred yards to the clearing.

"Okay, what are our options?" Jenna asked, feeling oddly calm despite the fact they'd been hit at least twice, and could be hit again. "There has to be another way."

She flew over the area where the troops were located, although she couldn't spot them beneath the canopy of the trees. Then she saw it—a clearing no more than ten feet across. Too small to lower the helicopter into, but big enough for a medic to descend with a stretcher. The procedure would be risky and was generally used only as a last resort, but Jenna didn't see any other options.

"JTAC, I have a clearing about thirty feet to your east. If you can move your man to that location, we'll send in a medic with a stretcher."

"I'll go down," came a voice from behind her in the cabin.

Jenna pushed her goggles back and twisted around to see one of the young medics, Sergeant First Class Randy Morrison, leaning through to the cockpit. His face was set in grim lines. Behind him, the crew chief was already preparing the hoist.

Jenna nodded. "Roger that."

Laura turned to face the medic. "We'll hover long enough for you to get on the ground, and then we'll take off. You'll have two, maybe three, minutes to load the patient onto the stretcher and move him to the larger clearing where we'll pick you both up. Got it?"

Sergeant Morrison nodded. "Got it."

Specialist Baker, the door gunner, lay down suppressive fire as a deterrent to any insurgents, while Sergeant Morrison scrambled into a harness. Jenna moved the Black Hawk into a hover. Sixty feet below, the clearing looked ridiculously tiny. Even as she watched, she saw several figures move amongst the trees and her night-vision goggles clearly identified them as U.S. ground troops. There were six of them. Four of them carried a body between them, while the remaining two provided cover.

"Okay, I've got them in sight," Jenna said, maintaining her hover position. "Good luck, Morrison."

With the medic's harness attached to a metal hook on a thick wire cable, Sergeant Helwig began lowering him down using the winch, calling out his position as he descended. When he was about twenty feet above the ground, machine-gun fire opened on them from what seemed like every direction. A rocket-propelled grenade whizzed past the nose of the aircraft, so close that Jenna thought she could actually see the vapor trail it left. Her first instinct was to pull up on the cyclic stick and get the hell out of there, but she held the helicopter steady and prayed that Sergeant Morrison wouldn't be killed as he dangled on the wire.

"We're taking fire! We're taking fire!" Laura shouted through the headset. "Get that man on the ground!"

The crew chief worked the winch faster, while Specialist Baker stood over her, keeping an eye on the rescue operation unfolding beneath them.

Bullets chinked against the side of the helicopter and two rockets whizzed by as Jenna held the helicopter steady. Behind her, she heard Specialist Baker returning fire.

"Goalie, I'm coming in," Chance said, his voice firm and controlled in her ear.

Then he was there, his Apache sweeping in low over the trees and spraying the large clearing with machine-gun fire. Through her night-vision goggles, Jenna saw that a group of insurgents had been making their way along the edge of the clearing toward the tree line. Chance laid down enough ammunition to effectively stop their advance.

"Okay, he's down and he's clear!" shouted her crew chief, and Jenna quickly steered her helicopter out of the kill zone.

"Where are those rockets coming from?" she demanded. "T-Rex, is the extraction site clear?"

"That's a negative," Chance replied. "We're going in hot."

As Jenna circled the trees, she could see one Apache still hammering the ridge with missiles and machine-gun fire, while the second Apache—Chance's aircraft—targeted the Taliban who were attempting to cross the clearing.

"JTAC, what's your position?" asked Laura.

"We are unable to reach the extraction site!" the JTAC shouted. "Repeat, we are taking fire and are unable to reach the extraction site."

"Damn!" Jenna said. "Okay, I'm coming back around. Hook the stretcher to the hoist and we'll winch him up."

Jenna knew their situation was perilous, despite the fact that Chance and Teacup were relentless in hunting down and eliminating the enemy. She took up her previous hover position while the crew chief and gunner monitored the rescue.

"Okay, the patient is on the hoist!"

Sergeant Helwig had just begun winching the stretcher upward when machine-gun fire exploded all around them and Jenna heard the now-familiar pings of bullets striking the side of the helicopter.

"Shit! That one hit the tail rotor!" shouted Specialist Baker, leaning out the door to inspect the exterior of the helicopter. "We're okay! We're good, we're good!"

If the tail rotors were disabled, they would crash, likely killing everyone on board, as well as the wounded soldier who dangled helplessly beneath them. Jenna knew if they had any chance of rescuing the man, they had just one choice.

"JTAC, I'm pulling up and getting out," she informed the ground coordinator. "Tell Morrison we'll circle back around and pick him up."

"Roger that."

Jenna flew the helicopter straight up until the gurney had cleared the trees, and then swung away to the west, out of the kill zone and away from the fierce fighting.

"Stop! Stop!" her crew chief screamed into the headset. "The gurney's swinging! We're going to lose him! Go to a hover!"

With her heart in her throat, Jenna straightened the aircraft out and came to a full hover. They were still over the trees, but she'd been heading toward the river, where they could finish hoisting the soldier to safety with less chance of being blown to bits. But even here, they could be targeted by an enemy rocket.

"Get that man on board!" Jenna growled.

"We've got him! We've got him!" the crew chief yelled. "He's on board! Go! Go!"

Jenna needed no further encouragement. She angled the helicopter around and flew in low along the tree line, trying to make themselves as inconspicuous as possible as they circled around and came back to the tiny clearing to retrieve the medic.

"JTAC, we're going to drop another hoist for Morrison," she told the ground coordinator, but even as the words were spoken, another burst of gunfire peppered the aircraft.

"Get out! Get out!" the JTAC shouted.

Jenna's night-vision goggles picked up the sight of tracer fire, eerily bright in the darkness, and she realized that more insurgents were making their way across the clearing, shooting at her as she hovered over the trees. There would be no way she could stay in position long enough to drop a hoist and winch Morrison back up.

"JTAC, we need an alternate extraction site," she said into the headset. "The clearing is under fire. Repeat, we need an alternate extraction site."

The JTAC provided the coordinates for a landing site some three hundred yards to the west, on the opposite side of the river.

"How is Morrison going to reach the far side?" she asked.

"He said he's a strong swimmer," came the reply. "We have a unit on the opposite shore to provide cover. Rendezvous in eight minutes."

"Roger that."

As Jenna turned the helicopter toward the river, she took a second to glance back at the flight surgeon and the second medic, who were working frantically to stabilize the wounded soldier. She only caught a glimpse of his injuries, but knew that unless they got him into surgery quickly, he wouldn't make it.

"Hold on, buddy," she murmured under her breath. "Just a few more minutes and we'll be outta here."

But as they flew low over the river, more machine-gun fire erupted near the new landing zone, forcing Jenna to retreat.

"JTAC, we're under fire!" shouted Laura. "Where can we land?"

"A landing isn't possible!" came the reply. "Leave Morrison and get that soldier to a hospital."

"I am not leaving Morrison behind," Jenna replied tightly. "I'm coming back around."

But as she swung around, another helicopter was there before her, cruising low over the landing site and laying down enough suppressive fire that the entire riverbank seemed to explode with light.

"You're cleared to land, Goalie," came Chance's voice over the headset. "Sorry for the delay. We got held up back there."

Jenna smiled and, as the Apache provided cover, she brought the Black Hawk gently down. Her wheels had barely touched the ground when Morrison dived through the open door and into the cabin of the helicopter.

"We've got him!" Specialist Helwig called. "Let's haul ass!"

Jenna didn't need any further encouragement. She forced the helicopter into a steep climb, angling away from the danger zone and toward Kandahar, the location of the closest coalition hospital. The entire mission had lasted less than twenty minutes, and yet Jenna felt as if an eternity had passed since she and Chance had exchanged words on the tarmac. Only now that they were safely away from the battle, did she realize she'd been operating on pure adrenaline.

"T-Rex, our crew is on board and accounted for, and we are heavy one wounded soldier," Jenna said into her headset.

"Roger that," came the reply. "I'll escort you in."

Jenna just barely contained her surprise. She hadn't expected Chance to guide her all the way to Kandahar, although of course he would. She didn't know how to respond, so she simply acknowledged the statement and then directed her attention to the rescue mission being performed in the cabin behind her.

"How's he doing, Doc?"

"He's lost a lot of blood, but we've managed to stabilize him," came the grim reply. "He needs immediate surgery."

"I'll do everything I can to make sure he gets it," she promised, and pulled on the collective until the Black Hawk was at its maximum acceleration. At this speed, she could knock crucial minutes off their estimated time of arrival. She figured they'd been hit by enemy fire at least a half dozen times, but they'd been lucky;

they were still operational and every mile they covered was critical.

When the lights of Kandahar came into view, she listened as Laura radioed the control tower and was granted priority clearance to land. She thought she would feel thankful to reach the large base, and for the injured soldier's sake, she was. But there was another part of her that understood that this was where she would say goodbye to Chance. He would return to Kabul and she would remain at Kandahar.

As they closed the distance to the base, Jenna allowed herself to reflect on what Chance had said. Was he right? Had she been eager to fly this mission because she felt she had something to prove? Her first reaction was a vehement denial. Her father had never talked about his Vietnam experiences. She hadn't grown up listening to his tales of glory, and she'd never harbored any fantasies about doing something heroic. She'd made the decision to follow in his footsteps and become an army helicopter pilot simply because she loved to fly. At the time, it seemed the best way to make a living and continue to improve her piloting skills.

But now she acknowledged that there may have been some truth to his words. All her life, she'd struggled to gain her father's approval. Had she subconsciously hoped that by flying this mission, she would earn that? Or had there been a part of her that wanted to prove she was just as capable as her male counterparts? She wasn't sure she wanted to explore her reasons for volunteering for the mission.

They were flying over the perimeter of Kandahar Airbase now. In contrast to Sangin, this base was enormous and the airport was the largest in Afghanistan, servicing more than one hundred flights each day. As

she approached the landing zone, she saw a field sur-
gical team waiting to rush the wounded soldier into
surgery. She utilized every bit of training she had to
bring the big helicopter in as gently as she could, and
no sooner had her wheels touched the ground than the
flight surgeon and medics transferred the injured soldier to a waiting ambulance.

Jenna powered down the rotors and began the routine process of shutting the helicopter down. Her crew
chief and gunner both jumped out, pulling their helmets and protective vests off and tossing them onto the
cabin floor before they began circling the Black Hawk,
inspecting the damage. By the time Jenna removed her
own helmet and climbed out, they had been joined by
a half dozen maintenance crew, all of them circling the
helicopter with expressions of astonishment.

"We were pretty lucky," Specialist Baker commented, fingering a small divot in the paint, just beside
the cabin door. "We've counted fourteen bullet holes."

Jenna just stared at the other woman, speechless.
They'd been hit fourteen times, and yet none of those
strikes had inflicted any serious damage? That wasn't
just luck; that was a freaking miracle. But it wasn't
until she slowly made her way around the Black Hawk,
counting the holes, that she had a full appreciation for
just how lucky they were.

One of the bullets had passed less than a centimeter
from the hydraulic system that powered the huge helicopter. Another had penetrated the metal so close to the
fuel tank that Jenna couldn't believe it hadn't sparked
an explosion. For the first time since she'd climbed into
the cockpit to rescue the wounded soldier, she appreciated just how much danger they'd been in. She looked
quickly at the faces of the women around her; women

she would trust with her life. Women she *had* trusted with her life.

"Is everyone okay? Nobody hit?" Jenna had heard of instances where crew members had been shot and didn't realize it until later, or where a bullet had penetrated their body armor but hadn't inflicted any bodily damage.

"No, ma'am. We're all good," her crew chief replied.

"Sergeant Helwig, I beg to disagree with you." Jenna smiled. "You guys aren't good—you're the best. What you did up there was nothing short of amazing and I'm honored to have flown that mission with you."

"You sustained damage to the engine compressor," said one of the maintenance crew, peering down at her from on top of the helicopter. "You won't be flying any more missions in this baby until we get her repaired. She should be ready by morning."

Jenna nodded, thankful that there was an entire fleet of Black Hawk helicopters at Kandahar, so the troops wouldn't go without needed air support.

"Captain Larson, welcome back and congratulations."

Jenna turned to see her unit commander, Colonel Brad Tyler, standing several feet away. He was an imposing man, well over six feet tall, with steel-gray hair and eyes to match. Jenna had worked under him for nearly three years and she could count on one hand the number of times she'd actually seen him smile. He swept his gunmetal gaze over the women and Jenna was certain she detected something like pride in his eyes.

"Thank you, sir," she replied. "It's good to be back."

Had it really been only two days ago that she had departed Kandahar Air Base to transport troops to

Forward Operating Base Kalagush? It seemed a lifetime ago.

"I haven't seen the report yet," he continued, "but I've already heard what happened. All I can say is you have nerves of steel, Captain. Maintaining a hover position over those troops while taking that kind of enemy fire took real guts."

Jenna stood up straighter. "Thank you, sir, but I couldn't have done it without this crew. They were the ones who had the toughest job. They risked their own lives to bring that soldier and the medic back on board."

Colonel Tyler looked at each of the women in turn. "You should take pride in your actions tonight. You've done great credit to your battalion and to the United States Army, and thanks to you, we were able to save the life of that soldier. Well done." He turned back to Jenna. "Captain, I want a complete report on my desk by oh-six-hundred tomorrow."

"Yes, sir." As the Colonel walked away, Jenna shifted her attention to the two Apaches, fully expecting to see the pilots receiving their own nods of congratulation. Instead, it looked as if they were gearing up for another mission. Maintenance crews crawled over the aircraft and she could see them restocking the rocket barrels and machine guns, while a tanker truck refueled them.

She spotted Chance standing by the cockpit of his Apache, speaking with Fishhead, his copilot. Without giving herself time to change her mind, Jenna jogged the short distance to where they stood.

"What are you doing?" she asked without preamble, interrupting whatever discussion they had been having.

Chance wheeled around in surprise, but Jenna didn't miss how he swept his gaze over her as if assuring himself that she was in one piece. "Nice job up there, Captain," he said. He glanced at Fishhead. "I'll just be a minute."

Taking Jenna's elbow, he steered her toward the nose of the Apache, where there was less activity. "Listen," he began. "What I said earlier…about you wanting to prove yourself…" His jawline tightened. "I was out of line. What you did out there was truly spectacular. I don't know many pilots who could have handled that kind of combat situation with the skill that you did."

Jenna felt something in her chest shift. His words caused a warm glow of pleasure to spread through her. The fact that he hadn't invalidated his praise with the words *even though you're female,* or *especially considering this was your first combat mission* wasn't lost on her, either.

"Thank you," she said simply. "That means a lot to me."

"Yeah, well, I behaved like an ass and I apologize. You did a great job."

"You're going back out there." Her words were a statement, not a question.

"I have to. Those troops need air support or there are going to be more rescue missions before the night is over. As soon as we're rearmed and refueled, we're leaving."

Jenna nodded, because there wasn't anything she could say. This was his job, as much as going out to retrieve that wounded soldier had been hers. Asking him not to go wasn't an option.

"Well, watch your flank," she finally said. She had no idea if and when they would see each other again.

Chance nodded. "I will. You take care of yourself, okay?"

The finality of it all struck her and panic filled her. What if he was injured, or worse? She realized she hadn't come close to saying what was in her heart, and to leave those words unspoken might be the biggest regret of her life.

"Chance—" Her voice broke.

For just an instant, his face twisted. Then he hauled her closed and planted a brief, hard kiss on her mouth. She didn't even have time to register it or respond before he released her and stepped back.

"I'll see you later." Then he turned and walked away.

Jenna moved back from the landing zone and watched as the maintenance crew completed their preparations and Chance climbed into the cockpit. The rotors of the big helicopter began to churn, chopping at the air and stirring up clouds of dust. Jenna threw an arm over her nose and mouth as the two Apaches slowly rose into the air on a wave of thunder and heat, the *thwap-thwap-thwap* of the blades reverberating through her chest.

They hovered briefly and then dipped nose down as they accelerated forward. She wasn't certain, but she thought she saw Chance raise a hand in farewell just before the big Apache roared away into the night.

14

JENNA FELL INTO A FITFUL sleep sometime after midnight. She'd spent most of the evening at the flight ops shack, writing her official report of the rescue and listening to the transmissions coming in from where the ground troops were still pinned down by the Taliban. The two Apaches had been joined by other attack helicopters, and after nearly an hour had finally made progress in providing relief to the ground troops. Knowing that Chance was safe had been enough, and she'd stumbled to her quarters around ten o'clock, grateful to be back in her own CHU, in her own bed.

But sleep was elusive, and when it finally came, she dreamed of Chance. He was beside her in the narrow bed, his hard body pressed along her backside. She could feel his warm breath against her neck, and when he skated his fingers along her bare arm, he raised goose bumps on her skin. The dream was vividly real; she could even feel the hot, rigid thrust of his arousal against her buttocks and she sighed in pleasure. But when one hand slid around to cup her breast and run a thumb over her nipple, her eyes flew open in alarm.

Not a dream!

Panicked, she tried to jerk away, but a muscular arm restrained her.

"Shh, sweetheart, it's me." The voice was warm and husky in her ear. "It's just me."

Astonished and still blinking away sleep, she twisted her head to see Chance propped on his elbow behind her. Light from an outside pole filtered in through the small window of her tiny housing unit, providing just enough illumination to cast the room in silver shadow. But even in the dim light, she could make out his features. He looked tired, but there was no mistaking the heat of arousal in his translucent eyes.

"*Chance.* What…? How…? What are you doing here?"

"The firefight took longer than we anticipated. We got back about an hour ago, but I had some paperwork I needed to finish before I could come over."

He'd come to her straight from the battle. She frowned. "I mean, what are you doing *here,* in my quarters?"

He gave her a lazy grin and dropped a kiss onto her shoulder. "Making love to you, I hope."

Making love to her. She struggled to stay focused while his hand leisurely explored her beneath the loose T-shirt she wore. She'd heard stories about soldiers who came away from battle with a huge rush of adrenaline that they later described as being similar to sexual arousal. Maybe it was true, because right now Chance was definitely aroused.

"How did you know where to find me?"

"I asked."

Oh, God.

"Before you freak out," he continued, accurately interpreting her expression of horror, "I asked your copilot, Warrant Officer Costanza. Even then, I only asked if she knew where you were. She said you'd turned in for the night, and then proceeded to tell me exactly where your unit was located."

Jenna relaxed, secure in the knowledge that Laura would never tell anyone that Chance had spent the night with her. "I'm glad you're back." *And safe.* "I thought you might return to Sangin or Kabul."

He cupped one of her breasts and she arched helplessly into his palm. When he nuzzled the side of her neck, the roughness of his beard growth made her shiver.

"We escorted two Black Hawks back to Kandahar," he said against her ear, "but there's no way I could sleep in the visiting officer's quarters, not when I knew you were here, alone."

"Mmm, I'm glad you came." She shifted restlessly beneath his hand, and when his hot tongue traced the contour of her ear and bit down gently on the lobe, she turned in his arms until they were pressed together from chest to knee. It was only then that she realized he'd shucked his clothing and was completely nude. She swallowed hard and forced herself to concentrate, when all she really wanted was to grasp his thick length in her hand and rub herself against him. "I worried about you."

"You worried about *me?* Christ, lady, if you knew the hell I went through while you were lowering that medic…" His face grew dark at the memory. "I never want to go through something like that again."

"You did a great job covering me," she assured him, stroking the hand on her breast. "If it helps, there wasn't one point during that exercise where I was afraid for my own safety, because I knew you had my back."

He buried his face against her neck and his words were muffled. "Yeah, well I was scared shitless the entire time we were out there. I've never felt so powerless in my life. If anything had happened to you—"

His admission made Jenna catch her breath. "Hey, look at me."

He lifted his head, his expression raw.

"I'm okay," she whispered.

He searched her eyes for a long moment, and then covered her mouth in a deep, hot kiss that she felt all the way to her toes. Instinctively, she curled a leg over his hips and ran her free hand over his chest, reveling in the warm, hard muscles she encountered. He must have come straight from the showers, because he smelled of clean soap and a spicy deodorant.

He cupped her rear end in one big hand, urging her closer, even as he deepened the kiss, licking at her mouth and sucking on her tongue until she gave a moan of pleasure. His erection pressed against her stomach, hot and hard. He completely surrounded her until she became lost in the feel, smell and taste of him. When he tugged her T-shirt over her head, she raised her arms to help him and then tossed the garment onto the floor. There was an urgency to his lovemaking that demanded a response, and Jenna complied.

She tilted her head, welcoming the intrusion of his tongue, and used her own to explore his mouth. He tasted faintly of mint, and she used her teeth to bite gently on his lower lip, tugging on it until he gave a low growl and turned her onto her back.

Jenna caught her breath as he reared back on his knees between her splayed thighs. The indistinct light cast shadows over his toned body, emphasizing the thrust of bone and muscle and making her mouth go dry. His penis stood fully erect, thick and dark against the paler skin of his abdomen, and Jenna resisted the urge to reach out and wrap her fingers around his length. Her legs still bracketed his thighs, and now he reached down and swept her panties from her hips, pushing her knees back so that he could pull them completely free of her body. He tossed the scrap of silk aside, and Jenna silently thrilled to the masculine appreciation she saw reflected in his eyes as he stared down at her.

This was what she had wanted; what she *needed*.

She lay exposed before him like a sacrificial offering. His gaze swept over her, touching upon her breasts, her belly and the place between her legs where she thrummed with desire. Her own gaze drifted from his face to his impressive erection. It would take no more than a small adjustment of his position for him to enter her, and the inner muscles of her sex contracted hungrily at the thought. Reaching out, she stroked a single finger across the blunted tip, gratified when it came away slick with moisture. Capturing his gaze, she slowly put the finger into her mouth and sucked it, tasting his essence.

Chance's eyes grew dark, and he lay his hand flat on her chest. Jenna knew he must feel the uneven pounding of her heart against his palm. Slowly, he drew his hand downward, and Jenna's stomach muscles tensed beneath the heated contact. She held her breath, wanting him to touch her *there*. Instead, he used both hands to grasp her hips and pull her toward him so that her buttocks rested on his thighs. Then he leaned forward, sliding both hands upward, over the arch of her ribs until he captured her breasts.

Jenna gasped, her attention riveted on Chance's face

as he gently kneaded and stroked her pliant flesh, and then rolled her sensitized nipples between his fingers until they stood out in hard little nubs. His expression was rapt, as if he'd never seen her before; as if he got intense pleasure simply from touching her.

"Christ, you're gorgeous," he muttered.

Before she could protest, he slid his hands to her back and lifted her upward, supporting her weight as he bent and took a nipple into his mouth. Jenna sucked in her breath as his hot, wet mouth drew sharply on her, and she felt an answering tug of arousal in her womb. She threaded her fingers through his short hair, letting her head fall back as he laved first one breast and then the other with his tongue.

"Oh, God," she panted, "that feels so good."

He released her, allowing her to recline back against the pillows, and redirected his attention to her sex, where she pulsed hotly. He stroked his hands along her inner thighs, his expression almost reverent, before he brushed his fingers over her softness, barely touching her.

"Don't tease me," she whispered.

She ached for him to touch her. She wanted to squirm on his lap and drag his hand to where she needed it the most, but instead she lay pliant and still.

"Do you want me to touch you?" His voice was no more than a husky rasp.

"Yes, oh yes." Without conscious thought, she tilted her hips to give him better access.

"Oh, man," he groaned. "I'm trying so hard to go slow, to make this good for you, but I'm not sure—"

"I don't want you to go slow," she assured him, covering his hands with her own. "I want you inside me, fast and hard."

His expression grew taut. She watched, entranced, as he guided her hands to his rigid length and curled her fingers around his straining cock. His skin was satiny soft beneath her fingertips, but there was no mistaking the extent of his arousal; he pulsed hotly against her palm as she slowly stroked her hand along his length. He'd pulled her so close that her sex almost touched the base of his cock, and she imagined his reaction if she pushed upward and rubbed herself against his shaft.

He groaned loudly, and when Jenna glanced at his face, she saw that he'd tipped his head back and closed his eyes, his expression one of intense concentration. She wrapped her hand around the base of his shaft and cupped him from beneath, testing his weight in her hand. But when he used his own hands to guide her movements, she complied, watching the contrast of his strong, tanned fingers over her paler ones.

Watching him only heightened her own arousal. As she continued to stroke him with one hand, she slid the fingers of the other hand over herself, parting her folds until she found the small rise of flesh that ached and throbbed with need. As she skated her fingertips over her slippery clitoris, she was unable to prevent a small moan of pleasure from escaping her lips.

"Jesus."

Glancing up, she saw that Chance watched her through glittering eyes, his attention riveted to where she touched herself. Immediately, a hot rush of fluid drenched her fingers. Knowing that he watched her made her feel incredibly sexy. As she continued to stroke him with her free hand, she slid one finger inside herself, and then swirled the slickness over her labia, pausing to give her clitoris a little extra attention. She was so aroused…so close…

A low growl distracted her from what she was doing and she shifted her gaze upward. Chance's eyes were hot as he watched her, and now he took her hand and raised it to his lips, drawing her wet finger into his mouth and sucking on it. When he finally released her, Jenna felt as if he'd actually put his mouth on her *there*.

Before she could guess his intent, he leaned forward so that her legs dangled over his thighs, and grasped her hips in his hands. With one easy movement, he pushed inside her. Jenna gasped at the incredible sensation of fullness; at the sight of him rising over her on his knees as he thrust into her. He looked primal and utterly masculine. Pressure gathered and built at her core each time he withdrew and surged back into her.

"Look at me," he rasped.

Jenna did, enthralled by what she saw. His features were taut, his expression both possessive and tender. He moved over her and inside her, his muscles bunching and flexing with each movement. In that moment, he was pure, unadulterated male and he was all hers.

"I want you to come," he growled softly, smoothing one hand along the length of her body until he reached the apex of her thighs where they were joined. As he watched her face, he slid a finger over her sensitized flesh, making her arch upward with a helpless cry. "That's it… Come for me."

Jenna clutched at his arms, her inner muscles tightening around the thick slide of his penis until she could feel every push and drag of his flesh inside her. She was so close that another few thrusts would send her over the edge, but when he pressed his finger against her, she lost it. Wave after wave of bone-deep pleasure crashed over her, causing her to shudder and cry out.

As if he'd only been waiting for her orgasm, Chance

gave a deep groan and plunged into her. Jenna could actually feel him pulsing deep inside her as her body fisted around him. For several long moments, all she could do was lie there, chest heaving as she gasped for breath, her heart pounding hard against her rib cage. Chance was still on his knees with her legs splayed over his thighs, his head tipped back and his eyes closed as he dragged in air.

As Jenna watched him, she realized her worst fears were coming true—*had* come true. She'd fallen for Chance Rawlins. A helicopter pilot. A guy who would always put the mission ahead of her, because that was what he was supposed to do. What she was supposed to do, too. She didn't have time to dwell on her thoughts, however. In one movement, Chance lowered himself onto her and then rolled them both to their sides until they lay facing each other, her legs still encircling his hips. He stared at her for a long moment and then dipped his head to kiss her in a soft, moist fusing of lips that made her heart ache.

When he finally pulled back, he stroked her hair from her face and let his gaze drift over her features as if he would commit them to memory.

"What are you thinking?" Jenna asked.

He gave a rueful smile. "I'm thinking that you are the most amazing woman I've ever met. I'm wondering how I ever got lucky enough to walk out of that bar with you back in North Carolina, and then end up over here with you."

Jenna couldn't keep herself from laughing. "I'm not sure many people would think having sex in a modified shipping container is something to envy."

Chance chuckled and pressed his mouth against the base of her throat, where she knew her pulse still beat erratically. "I don't know. Right now I feel like the luckiest son of a bitch on the planet."

"Well, thanks," she murmured.

"And just for the record," he continued, using one finger to tip her face up, "I'm not just referring to the sex. I meant what I said. I think you're an incredible woman."

"Yeah, well, you're not too shabby, either," she responded lightly.

"Even for a pilot?" he asked, amusement lacing his voice.

Jenna met his eyes. "Especially for a pilot." She hesitated, wondering how much she should tell him. "I guess it's always been easier for me to just lump all pilots into the same category."

"By *easier,* you mean *safer.*"

Jenna chewed her lower lip and nodded. She didn't like acknowledging how narrow-minded she'd been. "Yes. I was afraid that if I got involved with a pilot, I might end up falling for him and then where would I be? I know better than anyone what kind of life a military pilot leads, and it isn't exactly compatible with the white picket fence and two-point-five kids."

He pulled back just a little and stared at her so intently that Jenna grew uncomfortable and averted her gaze.

"Is that what you want?" he finally asked. "A house in the suburbs and a family?"

"Yes. No." She rolled onto her back and stared at the ceiling of the little room. "I don't know. Eventually, I guess that's what I'd like."

Chance propped himself up on his elbow with his head on his hand and looked at her. "I'm not so sure."

Jenna turned her head on the pillow. "What do you mean?"

He shrugged. "I just think that if you had that kind of life, you'd be bored to tears within a couple of years. Don't get me wrong. I want a family someday, too. But I can't see myself ever giving up flying. It's in my blood. It's who I am. And it's who you are, too."

Jenna snorted. "Yeah, well, my father never gave up flying but that didn't mean he was happy. He made my mom miserable. The closest I've ever seen him to happy is when he's in the cockpit of a helicopter. I don't want that."

Chance traced his finger in a lazy pattern over her stomach. "I think your father battled a lot of demons," he finally said, his tone careful. "He gave everything he had to that war. He must have been scared shitless, but he kept drawing on whatever reserves he had to keep going back into battle to save those men. He gave that war everything he had, and in the end, maybe there wasn't anything left for anyone else. Maybe not even for himself."

Jenna smiled at him, but she could feel the edges of her mouth wobbling. "I suppose next you're going to say that in spite of all that, he really does love me."

To her surprise, Chance gathered her in his arms and pulled her against his chest, pressing his lips to her temple.

"Of course he does," he rumbled softly against her ear. "How could he not?"

15

WHEN JENNA WOKE UP the following morning, Chance was gone. She'd known he would be; there was no way he could stay and risk anyone seeing him leave her housing unit. Still, she lay on her narrow bed and ran her hand over the spot where he had lain just hours earlier. Her pillow still bore the imprint of his head, and so she buried her face against the cool cotton and breathed in his scent.

Glancing at her bedside clock, she saw it was just past 5:30 a.m. Her alarm wouldn't go off for another thirty minutes and she was content to lie there and recall the night she'd spent with Chance. He hadn't actually said that he loved her, but he'd implied it.

Hadn't he? He'd stated that of course her father loved her, as if he found it impossible that anyone—including himself—could *not* love her. Or was she reading too much into those words? Groaning, she turned on her side and bunched the pillow beneath her head. She no longer knew. He'd certainly *acted* as if he loved her.

And if the sex last night had been great the first time, it had been off-the-charts amazing the second time, when Jenna had woken Chance up by planting warm, damp kisses against his skin, starting at his jaw and working her way down the length of his body. By the time she'd reached his hips, he'd been wide awake, as evidenced by his growing arousal. She'd filled her hands and mouth with him and hadn't stopped until he'd lifted her away and turned her onto her stomach beneath him. Even now, she was deliciously tender from their lovemaking, and her muscles ached from the unaccustomed demands he'd made on her body.

Had he returned to the itinerant officers' quarters here on Kandahar, or had he already flown back to Kabul? He'd said he wouldn't leave without saying goodbye, but realistically she knew that might not be possible. They'd talked about seeing each other again, as much as they could until their deployments ended. They hadn't talked about what would happen when they both returned to the States, where she would rejoin her unit in upstate New York, and he would return to North Carolina. Military relationships were hard enough without the added difficulty of distance and future deployments. She just didn't see how they could make it work, but Chance had been determinedly optimistic.

Sitting up, Jenna swung her legs to the floor and scrubbed her hands over her face. If it was meant to be, then it would work itself out. But right now, there was very little about their relationship that she could control, so it didn't make sense worrying about it. Standing up, she scooped up her panties and T-shirt from where she'd tossed them during the night and shoved them in her laundry bag. She'd drop the bag off at the base Laundromat on her way to the gym. After showering and tidying her room, she pulled on a pair of shorts and T-shirt and was just shoving her feet into her sneakers when someone pounded on the door. Hard.

Her heart leaped in her chest, hoping it might be Chance. It was just past six o'clock in the morning, and she couldn't imagine who else might be trying to rouse her. But when she opened the door, a young sergeant stood at attention, his face expressionless. Adrenaline surged through her veins. Even as the thought exploded in her head, she knew the likelihood that he had come about Chance was remote.

"Ma'am, you're wanted in Colonel Tyler's office, ASAP."

"Do you know why?"

"I'm sorry, ma'am, but I don't."

"Okay, I'll be right there."

As she closed the door and stripped out of her fitness clothes, her mind played through all the possible reasons why Colonel Tyler might want to see her, and none of them were good. Had he somehow found out that Chance had stayed in her room? If so, she could kiss her career goodbye. She could accept that for herself, but there was no way she wanted Chance to suffer. He loved the military, and he loved his job as a helicopter pilot. If he lost that, they'd never have any chance at a relationship, because she would always be a reminder of what he'd given up.

She pulled on a clean uniform, swiftly laced her boots, and grabbed her weapon. As she made her way across the base, she mentally rehearsed what she would say to shift the responsibility of their actions to herself. She entered the commander's outer office and a female sergeant directed her to wait there. Jenna stood looking out the small window, furtively wiping her damp palms on her camo pants. She could see the helicopter landing zone, but was unable to tell how many Apache helicopters stood on the tarmac. Was Chance still on the base?

"Captain Larson? The colonel will see you now."

Jenna turned to find the female sergeant holding the colonel's door open for her. Setting her weapon aside, she drew in a deep breath and stepped into the commander's office. The door closed behind her. Colonel Tyler was bent over his desk, writing something, and he glanced up briefly as she entered.

"Have a seat. Captain," he said tersely, indicating a nearby chair.

Jenna perched on the edge of the seat and waited in tense anticipation as he finished what he was doing and then pushed his chair back. Standing up, he came around the edge of his desk. His expression was grim and Jenna felt her heart sink. *He knew.* There could be no other reason for his manner. Swallowing hard, she forced herself to remain poised and not fidget beneath his appraising stare.

"Did you get any sleep last night, Captain?" he asked.

Oh, God. He definitely knew. Why not get right to the point? Colonel Tyler was well known and respected for his direct manner, so why would he play games with her? Refusing to rise to the bait, she nodded.

"Yes, sir. As much as could be expected."

He sat on the edge of his desk. "Good. I remember the first time I had to fly a combat mission. I couldn't sleep for a week afterward. But you did a fine job last night and I'm pleased to say the wounded soldier you saved will survive."

Jenna nodded again. "That's good to hear, sir."

The colonel cleared his throat. "Jenna," he began, using her first name in a rare display of familiarity, "I have some bad news."

Jenna's pulse kicked into high gear. Was it Chance? His face was so grim that the news had to be very bad. She mentally braced herself, curling her hands into fists on her lap.

"I'm listening," she said.

"I received an emergency notification from the Red Cross. Your father suffered a massive heart attack several hours ago. He's alive, but he's not expected to survive. I'm very sorry."

Jenna stared at him for a long moment, trying to comprehend his words. Not Chance. *Her father. Dying.* She shook her head, not quite believing what she'd heard.

"I've arranged for you to return immediately," Colonel Tyler continued. "Just pack the essentials. I'm giving you authorization to take as much time as you need. There's a flight departing Kandahar in one hour for Kuwait, and from there you'll continue on to Fort Lee, Virginia."

"Thank you," she replied automatically. Standing up, she felt disoriented and numb. Her father couldn't be dying. He was Erik Larson, a man who had cheated death so many times that she'd believed nothing could harm him.

"For what it's worth, your father is a great man," Colonel Tyler said quietly. "He is one of the best pilots this country has ever seen and you should be very proud to be his daughter. I'm sure he is very proud of you."

"Yes," she murmured. "Thank you very much."

He gave her a slip of paper with the name of a Boston hospital. Her father must be in critical condition if they'd transported him to Boston instead of treating him at the small Cape Cod facility.

She went back to her housing unit to pack a bag, still

struggling to get her head around the fact that her father was dying. For all she knew, he could already have died. How long did they expect him to survive? And if he was still alive, would she make it back in time to say goodbye? Her vision blurred and she swiped furiously at her eyes. She wouldn't cry. If there was one thing she was certain of, it was that her father wouldn't want her to grieve for him.

"Captain Larson!"

Jenna turned to see Chance jogging toward her from the direction of the fight line. He wore his flight suit, and even in her distress, she couldn't help but admire how good he looked. He was lean and fit and tanned, and his pleased smile revealed the dimples she loved so much. But as he drew closer, his smile vanished.

"What's wrong?" he demanded. "You're crying."

He looked around as if he expected to see the source of her unhappiness standing nearby and fully intended to beat the crap out of whoever was responsible.

Jenna bent her head and continued walking. "I just came from Colonel Tyler's office."

Chance fell into step beside her. "What happened? What did he say? Because if it's about last night, I'll speak with him. I'll accept full responsibility. Christ, this is all my fault. You were sleeping—"

Jenna stopped and turned to face him, laying a hand across his mouth to halt his words. "This has nothing to do with last night," she assured him.

He pushed her hand away. "Then what is it? What could possibly make you this upset?"

Jenna blinked and looked away. "It's my father. He had a heart attack and isn't expected to survive. In fact, he could already be gone."

Her voice broke on the last word, and with a soft

groan of dismay, Chance hauled her into his arms. "Ah, sweetheart, I'm so sorry. When did this happen?"

"A few hours ago," she sniffed, her voice muffled against his shoulder. "I'm actually heading back to the States right now."

"Okay. I'll come with you."

Jenna pulled away, bewildered. "What? No. You can't come with me. They won't let you, and why would you want to, anyway?"

Grasping her shoulders, he looked directly into her eyes. "Because I care about you. Because I want to be there for you. I can probably get some home leave, especially if I explain our relationship."

Jenna gave a harsh laugh and shrugged his hands off before she continued walking in the direction of her CHU. "Oh, right. That should go over well with your commanding officer."

"I guess the question is, do you want me to come with you? If you do, then I'll do whatever it takes to make it happen."

Jenna turned to face him. His face was serious now, the dimples gone. She let her gaze linger on his features, memorizing the square cut of his jaw, the full sensuousness of his lower lip, his cheekbones and the proud thrust of his nose and, finally, his eyes, which always reminded her of the sea. Did she want him to come with her? More than anything. Did she want him risking his career to do so? Absolutely not.

"Listen," she said carefully, "it's not that I don't appreciate the offer, because I do. But there wouldn't be much you could do, and I'd rather you didn't reveal our relationship to the top brass. We don't even know where it's going from here."

His features tightened. "Really? I thought we'd figured that out last night."

"Yes, well, I'm actually reconsidering my future," she said, not meeting his eyes. "In four months, I'll be eligible to either recommit with the army, or get out altogether."

Chance frowned. "What are you saying? That you'd throw away a great career and return to civilian life? Christ, Jenna, you're scheduled to go before the promotion board in the spring. By this time next year, you could pin on major. You could have your own command—lead your own battalion."

"Not all of us dream of becoming heroes, Chance."

Chance stared at her. "Is that what you think? That I do this for the glory?"

Jenna thought of how he had protected her during the previous night's mission to save the wounded soldier. He'd been doing his job, and he'd likely receive no recognition or awards for what he'd done. More important, she knew him well enough to know that he wouldn't expect any decorations. As far as she was concerned, he was already a hero.

"No," she acknowledged quietly. "I don't think that. That's not what I meant. Look, I really should get going. I'll, um, be back in a couple of weeks and maybe I'll get a chance to fly up to Kabul, okay?"

Chance snorted. "Yeah. That sounds great." He blew out a hard breath. "I'm real sorry about your dad."

Jenna nodded. "Thanks."

They stood in awkward silence for a moment, before Jenna gestured vaguely in the direction of her housing unit. "I should probably—"

Before she could guess his intent, Chance stepped close and caught her face in his palms. He searched her eyes for a brief moment, and then lowered his mouth over hers in a kiss so incredibly sweet that Jenna thought she might start to cry again. When he finally pulled away, his expression was one of resignation and regret.

"You take care of yourself, okay?"

Jenna nodded. She couldn't speak for the hard lump in her throat. As she watched, he walked away. Her vision blurred and the edges of his silhouette wavered and distorted against the backdrop of desert and mountains, until he might have been no more than a mirage. Dragging in a deep breath, she turned and walked in the opposite direction.

16

JENNA RETURNED TO Kandahar Air Base just in time for Memorial Day, which seemed fitting, somehow. Had she really only been gone for three weeks? It seemed like an eternity. She had arrived in Kuwait the previous day and was fortunate enough to get a seat on a military flight headed to Afghanistan. Right now, as she watched Kandahar Air Base come into view on the ground below, she was glad to be a passenger and not the pilot. She would have had a difficult time keeping her mind on the task of flying. She looked down at the paper she held in her hands. How many times had she read it? At least a dozen.

Smoothing the creases, she reread it now, telling herself that this time she would not get weepy. But the fact that her father had written this letter to her nearly six years earlier, when she had first received her commission as an army officer, still stunned her.

When she had arrived at the hospital in Boston, Erik Larson had been alive, but in a coma. Jenna had maintained a near-constant vigil at his bedside until he slipped away almost a week later without ever regaining consciousness. He'd had numerous visitors, including a three-star general who, in a brief but solemn ceremony, had pinned a meritorious service medal to his hospital gown.

Her father had been buried with full military honors, and Jenna had been astonished at the number of high-ranking military members who had seen fit to attend the service. But the real surprise had come afterward, when she'd been contacted by her father's lawyer and told that he had left his helicopter tour business to her, as well as a substantial sum of money. He'd also left a generous amount for her mother, despite the fact she'd remarried years earlier. But all of that paled in significance when compared to the letter he had left for her. Jenna only wished he'd had the courage to give it to her while he'd been alive.

She sighed and folded the letter carefully before tucking it into the pocket of her camo jacket. In another few moments, she would be back at Kandahar, where she would resume her duties as a Black Hawk helicopter pilot. She'd had plenty of time to consider her career and her future options, and found herself replaying her last conversation with Chance over and over again in her head. A lot of guys might feel threatened by a woman whose career so closely mirrored their own. She knew for a fact that there were male pilots who felt that women had no place in the cockpit, but Chance wasn't one of them. Leave it to him to encourage her to stay and advance her career. His opinion mattered, and she found she didn't want to let him down. But neither could she see them having any kind of future if they were both stationed in different parts of the country or required to deploy, possibly at different times. They would be like ships passing in the night, and she just couldn't see a long-term relationship surviving that kind of separation.

Twenty minutes later, she had retrieved her duffel bag and made her way through the security checkpoint toward the military processing area.

"Captain Larson!"

Jenna turned to see Laura weaving her way through the crowds toward her. She smiled, happy to see her copilot.

"Hey, what are you doing here?" she asked, giving the other woman a one-armed hug.

"I figured you wouldn't want to wait for the bus, so I brought a car for you." Laura grinned. "We're just outside."

"You didn't have to do that," Jenna protested, but was secretly relieved that she didn't have to share the military bus with the dozens of other soldiers arriving at Kandahar.

"Yes, well, it was the least I could do. Besides, I was told that if you arrived before thirteen hundred hours then I was to bring you over to the headquarters office ASAP."

Jenna followed Laura outside, where the dry, baking heat of the desert momentarily took her breath away. Just three weeks of being back on the East Coast, breathing in the cool, salty air of the Atlantic, had been enough for her to almost forget the arid dryness of Kandahar.

She and Laura climbed into an armored Humvee that stood idling on the curb, with two armed soldiers riding in the front. "Why does the colonel want to see me?" Jenna asked, after she had stashed her backpack and duffel bag into the back and the Humvee began driving across the base.

Laura shrugged. "I think he's having a Commander's Call," she said, referring to the mandatory meetings that a commander periodically held in order to speak to his people.

"Has it been crazy while I've been gone?"

"No more than usual. I've been doing the Afghan shuffle, transporting people and troops back and forth, but I haven't been involved in any more rescue missions."

"Have you seen Major Rawlins?" She tried to keep her voice casual, knowing she failed miserably.

"Which one?" Laura asked archly. "Special Ops or Apache pilot?"

Jenna gave her a tolerant look. "Either."

"Oh, look," Laura said brightly, glancing at her watch. "We're already here, and not a minute too soon."

Looking out the window, Jenna saw they had arrived at the commander's headquarters, where both aviators and soldiers were already making their way inside. Climbing down from the Humvee, she smoothed her hands over her camo jacket and tucked a loose strand of hair behind one ear, wishing she'd had time to wash up and change into a fresh uniform. She'd been traveling for two days, and aside from feeling grungy and in need of a long shower, she felt jet-lagged and irritable. Blowing out a hard breath, Jenna grabbed her gear and followed Laura into the building to a small auditorium where the other soldiers were already taking their seats. Choosing a chair near the back, she dropped her duffel back onto the floor beside her.

The room was noisy with conversation and laughter and the scraping of chairs against the floor. Jenna could feel a headache coming on. Leaning forward, she pressed her fingers against her aching eyes and thought longingly of her quiet, air-conditioned CHU. She thought of Chance, who was located three hundred miles to the north and couldn't do anything to make her feel better. He hadn't tried to contact her while she'd been gone, and recalling their last conversation, she wondered if she had blown any chance of a real relationship with him. The thought made her feel even more depressed.

The room fell silent and Laura poked her hard on the shoulder. Looking up, she realized Colonel Tyler had entered the room. She rose quickly to her feet and stood at attention, her height affording her a clear view. The colonel stood with his aide, who held an armful of green folders and a stack of small, velvet boxes. An awards ceremony.

"Could the following individuals please come forward," he said without preamble. "Sergeant First Class Randy Morrison. Sergeant First Class Samantha Helwig."

Jenna gave Laura a meaningful look as the commander continued his roll call. She had a suspicion that she knew where this was going.

"Specialist Leeann Baker. Warrant Officer Laura Costanza. Captain Jenna Larson."

Jenna drew in a deep breath before she followed Laura to the front of the room, when all she really wanted to do was protest that this was some kind of mistake. She didn't know which award the commander was about to present, but she felt strongly that she had done nothing to deserve it. Feeling like an imposter, she fell into line beside her crew and fixed her gaze on a spot at the far end of the room. The colonel called out the names of the flight surgeon and the second medic who had performed the lifesaving emergency treatment on the wounded soldier, and Jenna watched as they made their way to the front of the room.

"Recently, these seven individuals standing before you put their lives at risk under enemy fire to rescue an injured soldier," Colonel Tyler said. "These men and women give great reassurance to our war fighters. They know that if push comes to shove, there are individuals who can provide the medical attention and evacuation procedures necessary to get them out of combat fast. Therefore, it is with great honor that I award each of these members the Bronze Star with Valor for their selfless and heroic actions."

He turned to Sergeant Morrison and Jenna heard him murmur words of congratulations as he pinned a medal onto Morrison's uniform and handed him the citation, before saluting sharply and moving on to Sergeant Helwig. When he reached Laura, a small group of men entered the auditorium and made their way to the back row. Jenna glanced at them, and then did a double-take as she saw they were pilots. Her heart leaped, but in the next instant she realized none of them was Chance. Then there was no further opportunity to look, since Colonel Tyler stepped directly in front her.

"Congratulations, Captain Larson," he murmured, pinning the heavy medal onto the front of her uniform. "That was some great flying you did out there. You're more like your father than you realize." He clapped her on the shoulder. "Welcome back. After this, why don't you go get some sleep? You look as if you could use it. Report to me at oh-seven-hundred tomorrow morning."

Jenna saluted smartly. "Thank you, sir."

Colonel Tyler finished pinning on the last medal and turned to face the auditorium. "Please join me in congratulating each of these deserving men and women, and then join us for a Memorial Day barbecue behind the headquarters building, where I understand the top brass is serving up ribs and corn on the cob."

The room erupted in cheering and clapping, and after shaking hands with her crew, Jenna searched the crowd for Chance. When she didn't see his tall form, she turned away, trying to hide her disappointment. There was no reason to expect that he would be here at Kandahar. She hadn't had any contact with him during the three weeks she'd been gone, and it wasn't as if he knew she would return today. He was at Kabul Air Base, three hundred miles away, and the likelihood that she would see him again anytime soon was pretty remote. Her hand slipped into the pocket of her jacket, feeling the letter that she had tucked there during the flight. She needed to make a decision and she needed to do it soon.

She felt someone bump her shoulder and turned to see Laura grinning at her. "Hey, did I hear Tyler give you the day off?"

Jenna shrugged. "I probably look like hell—he felt bad for me."

Laura snorted. "You look great, and he definitely has a soft spot for you. C'mon, let's go get something to eat."

Casting one last look around the room, Jenna blew out a hard breath and forced herself to smile. "Yeah, that sounds good."

Food was the last thing she wanted. Right now, all she longed for was her cool, air-conditioned CHU, a shower and her bed. But she didn't say so. Instead, she followed Laura outside to the parade field, where the base routinely held recreation events for the coalition forces. Several enormous tents had been erected to provide some protection from the sun, and the highest-ranking officers on the base were busy dishing out burgers, ribs and corn at tables set up as serving stations. The lines of soldiers stretched two hundred deep, and Jenna knew it would be a long wait.

Other soldiers labored over massive barbecue grills, flipping burgers and hot dogs. A stage had been erected on the back of a flatbed trailer decorated with red, white and blue ribbons and bows, and country music blared from two large speakers. A group of young men entertained the troops with their version of a country line dance, while twenty or more soldiers, both male and female, danced under a nearby tent. Stretched over the makeshift stage was an enormous banner that read We Love U.S.A.

A large cargo plane screamed overhead as it made its final approach to the Kandahar airstrip, and in the distance, Jenna could hear the distinctive *thwap-thwap-thwap* of at least two military helicopters. The entire scene had an almost surreal feel to it, since nearly all of the men and women surrounding her were in uniform, and all of them carried weapons.

"Pretty nice gig, right?" asked Laura, as they stepped into one of the long lines. She rubbed her hands together. "I can already taste those ribs!"

The line was barely moving, and the outside temperature was well over one hundred degrees. Jenna's uniform felt heavy and hot, and instead of giving her an appetite, the smell of the food made her a little queasy.

"You know what?" she said, putting a hand on Laura's shoulder. "I left my duffel bag back in the auditorium. This line is hardly moving, so I think I'll bring my gear to my room and grab a quick shower, and then come back."

Laura frowned. "You sure? Do you want me to get something for you?"

"No, but thanks. In fact, you'll probably still be standing here when I get back."

"Okay, then. See you in a few."

Jenna turned away, grateful to escape the pressing crowd and the noise, but she could feel Laura's concerned eyes on her as she made her way to the auditorium. The big room was empty now, and the awards ceremony might never have occurred, except for the weight of the medal hanging from the front of her uniform. Hefting her duffel bag over her shoulder, she made her way slowly across the base to her housing unit. Her boots kicked up dust as fine as talcum powder in the desert heat so that by the time she reached her CHU, she was coated in the stuff.

Inside, however, her room was cool and dark and she dropped her gear onto the floor with a grateful sigh. She wanted to flop onto her bunk and sleep until the next day, but unless she washed the sweat and dust from her hair, she'd only end up having to wash her sheets and blankets, as well. She carefully removed the Bronze Star medal from her uniform and placed it on the shelf next to her bed. Then, stripping out of her clothes, she walked naked to the tiny bathroom at the back of her CHU and turned the shower to a lukewarm spray. Standing underneath the water, she shampooed her hair and quickly scrubbed the travel dust from her skin. She knew she should conserve water and keep her shower short. Instead, she allowed herself the luxury of standing for several long minutes just letting the water sluice down her body.

Only when the water turned from lukewarm to cold did she finally turn it off and step out. Grabbing a towel from the nearby hook, she pressed it against her damp face and neck as she walked back into the living area, and came to an abrupt halt.

Chance lay sprawled on her bunk, larger than life, his arms bent behind his head as he watched her. He still wore his flight gear, which told her he had just completed a mission. The knowledge that he hadn't taken the time to strip out of the survival vest before he came to her CHU sent a thrill of pleasure through her, and it took all her restraint not to throw herself on top of him.

"Chance." She clutched the towel against her chest, knowing it did little to hide her nudity. "You're making a habit of catching me out of uniform."

His eyes gleamed. "You bet."

"You caught me by surprise."

"Really? I'd say I caught you at a perfect time. In fact, it's better than perfect because I don't have to be back on the flight line until tomorrow morning, and your copilot told me you have the rest of the day off." He studied her face. "How are you, Jenna?"

Jenna wrapped the towel around herself as best as she could without revealing too much, aware that it barely covered her breasts and bottom. Even as her entire body vibrated with awareness, she became aware of the small changes in him since she had last seen him. Although his eyes were warm as they traveled over her, Jenna thought he looked weary.

"I'm doing okay. But what are you doing here?" she asked, pushing a strand of wet hair back from her face. "I expected you to be at Kabul."

"I was, but I heard there was an awards ceremony today." Stretching his arm over his head, he picked up her medal from the shelf and admired it. "This is some seriously nice jewelry."

Walking over to him, Jenna touched the bronze star where it lay in his palm. "Thanks, although I'm not sure I deserve it. Any other pilot would have done the same thing."

"Maybe," he conceded. "But they didn't. You did." Still holding the medal, he closed his hand around hers until the bronze star was pressed between their hands. He drew her down until she sat perched on the edge of the mattress by his hip. "You earned this, sweetheart. Never think that you didn't."

Jenna raised her head and looked at him as he lay back against her pillow, and the expression on his face stole her breath. Without conscious thought, she leaned forward, her gaze dropping to his mouth. More than anything, she wanted to kiss him, to feel his lips beneath hers. He grew still. A droplet of water fell from her hair and splashed onto their joined hands, breaking the moment. Jenna pulled back, her breathing a little uneven. Slowly, Chance opened his fingers and released her hand, before replacing the medal on her shelf.

"Why don't you get out of that vest?" Jenna suggested, eyeballing his flight gear. She knew firsthand how uncomfortable the harness and survival vest were.

"Is that an invitation?" he asked softly, a crooked smile lifting one corner of his mouth.

Yes.

"Here, stand up and I'll help you," she said, rising to her feet. She watched as Chance stood up and began unfastening the vest, and then helped him shrug it off and drape it over a nearby chair. "Now, unzip that suit."

Her fingers went to his flight suit, but his hands

covered hers, stopping her. She looked up at him in surprise.

"Jenna, sweetheart," he groaned. "I volunteered to escort a transport helicopter from Kabul to Kandahar because I knew you were returning today, and I needed to see you. I'm trying to behave myself, but—" He gave a strained laugh and scrubbed a hand over his face as he raked her with one heated look. "You're making it real hard."

"Well, I certainly hope so," she murmured, letting her gaze drop pointedly to his crotch.

"Jesus." He laughed, and before Jenna could guess his intent, he caught her by the shoulders and pulled her toward him, searching her face. "God, I missed you."

He kissed her, a slow, deep kiss that had Jenna sliding her arms around his shoulders and straining to get closer. He buried his hands in her wet hair to gain better access, and Jenna heard herself moan softly in pleasure. She slid her tongue against his, reveling in the hot, slippery feel of him. When Chance finally lifted his head, she felt a little disoriented and clutched at his shoulders for balance.

"I hated the way we left things," she admitted, searching his eyes. "But I did a lot of thinking while I was gone, and I made some decisions."

"Come here," he muttered.

Jenna made no protest as he pulled her onto the bed and lay down beside her, tucking her against his side. Her towel rode up over her thighs and she tried unsuccessfully to tug the edge down again.

"Leave it," Chance said. "I like the view."

There was something arousing about the fact that he still wore his flight suit while she was naked beneath the towel. As she looked down the length of their bodies, her legs appeared slim and pale against the fabric of his olive jumpsuit. Jenna couldn't resist rubbing her foot along the length of his leg. He gave a soft groan and turned to press a kiss against her temple.

"You'd better talk fast," he growled softly.

"I love flying helicopters," she began, "and the military has enabled me to do that beyond my wildest dreams. But when I was out there that night, helping to bring that wounded soldier in, I had a taste of what my father must have experienced when he flew in Vietnam."

Chance grunted.

"After we buried my dad, I was going through the paperwork for his helicopter charter business and I found a letter that he wrote to me when I first received my commission." She paused. "You were right, Chance. He really did love me."

"Of course he did," Chance murmured, kissing her forehead. "What did the letter say?"

Jenna sighed. "So much. He wanted me to know how proud he was that I had chosen to follow in his footsteps, but more than anything, he wanted me to be happy. He said that he made a mistake leaving the military, and he always regretted it."

Chance lifted his head to look down at her, his face sympathetic. "That's tough."

"Yeah. He left because his family wanted him home, even though he wanted to stay in. Anyway, it got me thinking about the reasons why I joined the military in the first place, and I realized that, as much as I love flying helicopters, I became a Black Hawk pilot because I thought it would make my father happy." She was silent for a moment. "I've had a great career and I'll always be glad I joined, because if I hadn't then I would never have met you. But I've decided to put in my paperwork and get out."

Chance looked stunned. "You're kidding."

"I know this must seem sudden, but when I was home, everything fell into place. I love Cape Cod. I love working with the public, and I want to take over my dad's helicopter tour business."

Chance gave a disbelieving laugh. "I don't know what to say. You're a great pilot, Jenna. Are you sure about this?"

"Absolutely. But I won't give up flying Black Hawks entirely. I thought I might join a National Guard unit."

"Do you think a weekend a month and two weeks every year is going to be enough?"

Jenna smiled. "I think it will provide the balance that I've been looking for. This way, I can keep my certifications current, but I'll have time for…other things."

She was unprepared when Chance rolled onto his side to face her. His features were taut as he kissed her, and Jenna arched against him, silently telling him she wanted more. Chance dragged his mouth from hers.

"You should know that I've done some thinking while you were gone, too," he rasped. "My current commitment is over in a year. Last week, I contacted my recruiter and requested an assignment as a test pilot in Connecticut."

Jenna gasped. She didn't ask if he was serious, because she could see by his face that he was. "But you chose your unit at Fort Bragg so that you could be closer to your brother. Why would you go to Connecticut?"

He gave her a lopsided grin. "Why do you think?" He shrugged. "The military needs test pilots for the new Apaches and I need to be closer to you."

Jenna knew the Apache helicopters were manufactured in Connecticut. The army maintained a full contingent of active-duty pilots at the facility, their only job to take the newly minted helicopters on rigorous test flights to ensure they were fully operational before the military would agree to buy them. As a test pilot, Chance would work a more or less nine-to-five job, and have many weekends free.

"Oh my God. I can't believe it. Will you be happy doing that?"

"Sweetheart," he growled, "I will be ecstatic doing that, because it will mean I can spend time with you." He smiled wryly. "Of course, when I requested the assignment, I thought you'd be with your aviation unit in upstate New York, but Cape Cod works even better."

"So, you'll be just a few hours from where I'll be," she mused.

"Yes, ma'am. We can spend weekends together, and I can get time off to come up and help you out with the charter business, if you'd like."

"Won't you miss the excitement of flying combat missions?"

Chance was thoughtful. "I've flown more than one hundred combat missions. The real thrill comes from knowing you supported your guys on the ground, or helped to stop the insurgency. As a test pilot, I'll help ensure that the military gets the best helicopters possible to perform those missions."

"How long would the assignment last?"

"Three years, and while there's a chance I could get deployed during that time, we'll at least be able to see each other on a regular basis." He stroked the back of his knuckles over her bare arm. "What about you? Will operating a charter business make you happy?"

"There are some things I'll miss about the military,

but that's why I think joining the National Guard is a good choice. I'll still get to fly Black Hawks, but I'll also be able to have a personal life. I love Cape Cod and the islands," she said, smiling. "Some of my best memories are of the summers I spent flying charters with my dad, so yes, I think this will make me happy. But you know what I'm looking forward to the most?"

"What's that?"

"Not having to hide our relationship. I think part of the reason I avoided men in uniform is because subconsciously I was holding out for a hero—someone like my father, but without all the baggage. Someone like you."

"Sweetheart," he growled softly, rolling over and pinning her to the mattress, his eyes hot and glittering, "I don't consider myself a hero, but if you want me, then I'm all yours."

"Oh, I want you," Jenna assured him in a sultry whisper, tugging the towel free from her body. "Here, let me show you how much. But I warn you…this mission could be dangerous."

"Bring it on," he growled softly, nuzzling her neck. "I'm more than ready. For now and for always."

* * * * *